## About the Author

Born in Lucerne in 1946, Maria Caviglia grew up in Switzerland and, after that, spent over twenty years in Germany.

In 1993 she went on a cruise with her partner, skipper Erich. They bought the boat in the United States and sailed up the east coast to Canada and back to the south near Key West.

Then they sailed for five years in the Caribbean, went through the Panama Canal, and spent six years in the south Pacific.

After twelve wonderful years of sailing, they sold the sailboat in New Caledonia and returned home to Switzerland with countless memories.

Switzerland is still Maria's home.

Maria Caviglia

# DRUG SMUGGLING

AUSTIN MACAULEY
PUBLISHERS LTD.

Copyright © Maria Caviglia (2015)

The right of Maria Caviglia to be identified as author of this work has been asserted by her in accordance with section 77 and 78 of the Copyright, Designs and Patents Act 1988.

All rights reserved. No part of this publication may be reproduced, stored in a retrieval system, or transmitted in any form or by any means, electronic, mechanical, photocopying, recording, or otherwise, without the prior permission of the publishers.

Any person who commits any unauthorized act in relation to this publication may be liable to criminal prosecution and civil claims for damages.

A CIP catalogue record for this title is available from the British Library.

ISBN 9781784556938 (Paperback)

www.austinmacauley.com

Published (2015)
Austin Macauley Publishers Ltd.
25 Canada Square
Canary Wharf
London
E14 5LQ

This crime story, 'Drogenschmuggel' was published with a similar text in 2013 in German under the ISBN: 978-3-9524120-0-8

Printed and bound in Great Britain

This is a work of fiction. Names, characters, businesses, places, events and incidents are either the products of the author's imagination or used in a fictitious manner. Any resemblance to actual persons, living or dead, or actual events is purely coincidental.

# Touch of Fear

Black and pointed, reef tips threaten whoever dares to approach them. They are coming dangerously close to us and I am worried about the flawless hull of our sailboat.

I feel like I'm at the dentist: when will the nerve start shrieking, now? *Now?*

I bend far over the rail and try to estimate the depth of the water, and also, the distance from the cliff. This is a mighty narrow passage!

Up front, from the bow, I can see everything in the water very clearly, and — with appropriate hand signals — manoeuvre Alex past the danger. However, since my skipper must keep watching our sails, the wind and the tiller at the same time, he cannot always see my gestures very well.

Irritated, he orders me to use acoustic signals instead.

"Oh well, then," I shout back as an obedient navigator, "ten degrees to port — straight ahead — ten degrees — to port again, even more — now just straight ahead."

Finally, we are in the dark blue, and hence the deeper waters of the Caribbean Sea, beyond the reef belt.

"Phew, Alex, this passage through the reef is always an adventure, isn't it?"

"As is our entire trip together, my dear Sandra," he grins at me with his crooked smile, "do you regret it?"

"The adventure or the closeness with you?" I smirk, and return his smile with my bluish gaze.

Regret? Why should I regret all this?

As far as I am concerned, this trip could go on forever like this, with my good Alex by my side and our sailboat, the "Seeschwalbe" — our home.

Now, Alex lets the fishing line run out into the water over the rail, and soon it tightens. The bait sizzles through the waves with a silvery shine. Eventually, we hope for something good to eat, right here, coming out of the water. We have also decided, that is, my skipper has decided, to sail a few miles out into the open sea from the Ambergris Cay mooring site, and to try our luck out there.

Alex activates the autopilot, checks the sails, and soon we are sitting comfortably at the rail, him with a beer in his hands and me with a fresh fruit juice.

We gaze at the shore of Ambergris near Belize, and I use my binoculars for assistance.

Palm trees, mangroves, small patches of beach, more palm trees...

Alex flits into the cockpit from time to time to check the fishing line and the autopilot system. Spellbound, I look at this marvellous world.

The Caribbean sun blazes down on us from a bright blue sky. It is already very warm. Above our heads, pot-bellied pelicans trace their leisurely path through the air. Criss-crossing gulls rush past us, shrieking. As a counterpart to the creatures in the sky, glistening dolphins glide through our bow wave in the water, gazing at us now and then with tilted heads.

Alex sits down in the cockpit and empties his beer. His angular body leans against a cushion, relaxed, and his brown eyes contentedly look up at the sky.

The boat moves on without hurry, and I crouch there and allow myself to be enchanted by the sight of this fascinating peninsula.

Palm trees, beach, mangroves, small cove ...

But...wait a second! There, something inappropriate is interrupting the steady harmony of this gentle coastline. A movement? A pattern that does not fit here?

Suddenly, I imagine a haze of fear lying above the small cove we have just passed.

Instinct? Imagination? Fantasy?

"What the hell...?" Quickly, I grasp my binoculars more firmly and adjust them more precisely.

There, I see two young girls with a wooden boat. At first, they were digging around in the sand, but now they get up in a hurry and stare across the cove.

Just at this moment, a motorboat is making for the cove from the opposite side. It races towards the beach and heads directly for the girls. Four men climb out onto the beach before their boat has even come to a stop properly.

The girls have also started moving. They are running as fast they can. It seems they are running in panic for their lives.

The danger is perceptible. This is not my imagination. Inexplicable fear creeps up on me like an ice-cold breath, and the binoculars tremble in my hands.

"Alex!"

Because our sailboat has passed the small cove, I can now barely see the girls anymore. The last thing I still see through the palm trees on the corner of the headland is them disappearing into the mangroves. Boiling hot, it occurs to me: hey, we know these girls. We met them at San Pedro on Ambergris.

"Alex!" I shout. "Alex, my God, come here!"

But Alex does no such thing. Slowly and carefully, he reels in his fishing line, as he has just caught our lunch.

"Alex, please!" I feel like I am going to cry.

"Just a minute, I can't let this fine fellow run away – I mean swim away! Better that you help me! "

How can he! Because of a stupid fish!

But if I deny him my help, this will go on even longer. With lightning speed, I am there with Alex, helping him to bring in the fish and lay it on the deck. With a hard blow, Alex releases the fluorescent golden mackerel from its suffering. Without any hurry, he wants to start...

"Alex!" My tone leaves no doubt about the urgency. "Now, you come and look at this cove and the girls."

"Girls are always good," Alex murmurs, but my bad look makes him fall silent.

Together we crouch on the rail and scan the coastline, me with my naked eye and Alex now with my binoculars.

"Palm trees, mangroves, sandy beach, and more palm trees," Alex mutters impatiently, and passes the binoculars back to me.

"Yes, of course, we are already too far south. By the time you had finally reeled in your fish..."

Muttering – I would have liked to have understood what he was saying – Alex walks back to the cockpit, works on the sail setting and the autopilot and makes a turn. Then, he controls everything carefully and comes back again to the foredeck. We both change to the other side of the boat and look at the shore again.

Palm trees, beach, mangroves, cove...

"Here! Here is the small cove," I quickly pass the binoculars to Alex. I can still see well enough without them. The cove, the motorboat, the small wooden boat beside it — and the men, four men, who just now disappear into the mangroves.

"No girls?"

"No, Alex, the girls have run off, into the mangroves."

"And you think...?"

"Yes, run off in panic."

Alex looks at me doubtfully "You could see *this*?"

Really mean, that's how his incredulous tone sounds.

"Yes, we must do something!"

"We can't go back to Ambergris anymore today. Look at the clouds up there. The reef entrance is too dangerous without having a good view."

I also know this. Furious, I look at the clouds, but they do not want to give way.

Alex is right. It does not look good for a journey along the prongs of the cliff.

He says, "But we can go to the small Cay Caulker Island. This is not so far. What do you think? There, the entrance channel is much easier to navigate. And then, as early as possible tomorrow, we will immediately go to…"

"Good, and then also go back to Ambergris as soon as possible tomorrow."

As soon as possible, ok, but won't that be too late?

But Alex is the skipper after all — he has the say.

What would I decide in his place? Going with the boat into the small cove is clearly not possible, as there is no passage through the reef with enough depth for a sailboat keel. Going back to Ambergris also does not work, because of the poor visibility.

And I myself? What should I do? Hop from the boat and swim over?

Sandra, Sandra, I scold myself, you wouldn't be able to help at all. Against these men, you wouldn't stand a chance.

So, I concede the need for obedience: the skipper's decision is right.

I wonder whether we will find the girls tomorrow in Ambergris? What might have happened? It is not fine with me at all, the thought that somewhere out there, they are in danger.

"We could report it to the police on the radio."

My skipper looks at me questioningly. "Didn't you see the police uniform? On one of the men? What are you thinking, suggesting that?"

"Oh, Alex, of course I saw it. The policeman was just running after them. What else is there to think?"

"Maybe the girls were not allowed to bathe there and the police chased them away?"

"These were no brats! I recognized both girls. They were Kati and Biene, whom we met at the resort …"

"The two beautiful, slim ones, with the long legs?"

"Yes."

"You were able to recognize them? From here?"

"I think so…"

"Tomorrow, we'll go to the resort and you will see, your fanta…I mean your fears…"

"I think you wanted to say fantasies?"

"Will dissolve into nothing. And the girls will be in good spirits after experiencing their best holiday adventure yet. Hunted by police."

"Oh, Alex, just put a sock in it."

# Carefree at Cay Caulker?

Just how I like it. Seated in my favourite corner in the cockpit and cuddling up into soft cushions, I listen to the soft jingling of the rigging. I close my eyes and immerse myself in the familiar tune. With each beat of the metal parts on the mast, fine ringing tones vibrate through the warm air. Then I have to smile because, to me, these sounds seem like the ringing of cow bells in the mountains of my native country, Switzerland. Immediately, I conjure up images of cows on juicy pastures, of green meadows laced with flowers and with small, babbling brooks running through them.

But as soon as I open my eyes, the green outline of the rows of palm trees whisks me back from the beautiful mountains into the equally beautiful Caribbean world.

"Seeschwalbe" lies softly bobbing up and down at anchor in the protected cove at Cay Caulker, where we arrived from Ambergris. It is much easier to come in here, even with less good light.

But fear for the safety of the girls catches up with me again. If only we're not going to be too late tomorrow!

But this is just the way in this island world. You cannot quickly hop into the car or take a bus and get help. You have the sailboat, and so, you are then very exposed out on the sea, and very limited in mobility.

A few clouds and you cannot get behind the reef; a little wind or waves and you see no shallows and corals in the water. Then, you simply have to remain in a safe place.

And the radio? Who would listen to us here? The police, who were also there in the small cove; Or at least one policeman. How reliably can we get assistance for the girls from them? Then, they would immediately know that we had seen something — something we weren't supposed to see. Really, it's better that we wait until tomorrow.

Also, we cannot ask anybody on the island for help. A few fishing boats are at anchor beside us, but I do not see a soul. On the banks, there are also no houses or huts. If people do live on the other side of the island, we don't know if we can trust them.

The wind picks up again. A few clouds are billowing in the West, dark and looming. They lump together and become black. Before we have even taken our cushions and sea charts below deck, and rolled up the sun roof, the first heavy drops of rain hammer down onto our boat. A heavy tropical rainstorm rushes over the area.

How fast this can happen.

Quickly, I close the hatches leading onto the deck and open the inlet of the water tank. I watch, transfixed, as the water runs over the deck and shoots through the strainer into the opening. Ten minutes, maybe fifteen, then it bubbles up from the hole; our water tank is full. So, we are well supplied with the precious liquid once again. Hardly have I opened the right inlets again, than I close them when the rain stops, as though a tap in the sky had been turned off. The clouds break up and the sun shines down on us, as though nothing has happened. Within about twenty minutes, everything is dry again.

Such a tropical thunderstorm is impressive. Like a visitation, it descends upon us once or twice a week, fills the tank for us, washes the boat clean and is gone again in no time.

A light wind is now ruffling the turquoise waters, gliding over the sailboat and over the cove up to the white beach, where it sends gentle waves onto the sand. In the deep blue sky, I can see no more trace of clouds. I shield my eyes against the sun and look over to Ambergris Cay. On the dark-green strip of land, I can see a few cottages lit up, and the white church tower and the radio mast and telephone poles sparkling in the evening sun, as though in competition with each other for the most splendid light.

"Alex!" I call out as the waves go down, "We could now find our way into the reef OK."

Alex sticks his head out of the hatch and examines the sky, before muttering laconically, "Now yes, but not earlier. And now it's too late. The sun is already too low on the reef. By the time we get there, it will be dark."

I also mutter something to myself, which, fortunately, he doesn't understand.

"Don't complain now, girl. Tomorrow, as early as possible..." and then he disappears into the saloon.

So, I bring up the cushions and my book again and sit down in my corner of the cockpit. There is still a little rainwater in the grooves of the wood bench. But that doesn't bother me. I lay down a cushion and snuggle into it.

I can't concentrate on reading as my thoughts keep turning to the girls, Biene and Kati. I'm trying to recapture what I actually saw in the small cove:

Two girls are kneeling beside a wooden boat; they are startled, jump up and run away. A few men drive into the cove in a motorboat. One of the men wears a police uniform. The girls are running away in panic.

Panic? Could I really make out panic from that distance? Certainly not in their faces, but in their movements, the way they had been running away in a panicky manner. But when we went back, Alex and I could only see the men, who disappeared into the mangroves at the end of the beach.

And the girls? Had I really been able to recognise them? Hardly their faces. And their likeness? Clearly.

There probably aren't two other such girls on the Ambergris peninsula or throughout Belize. With long, blonde hair, slim — and white. And so close to the resort where the girls are on their holiday? Hardly. There are coincidences in life, but so many in one place?

When I conjure up the image of the running girls in my head, then I think I have even recognised their different personalities.

Externally, the two of them resemble each other. The slim figures, the long blonde hair and the light skin are their most striking features.

But the similarity stops there. Kati's gentle face, her fine, silvery hair, her little smile and her usually quiet voice are the image of her reserved personality. Only her friend, Biene, seems to be able to entice the shy girl out of her reserve, and incite fun and frolic into her.

Biene's unruly locks of hair, her round face with honey-coloured skin and the sweeping lips, always twisted into broad laughter, display a pure joy in life and an open, cheerful character.

I recognised these exact differences in the girls, who were running away.

Kati's hesitant movements when fleeing, her frightened looking back over her shoulder and the nervous dangling of her arms and legs stood in stark contrast to Biene charging ahead. She had stomped off like a steamroller, her goal firmly in mind, not looking to the left or right. I wonder if both escaped, the hesitant one and the daredevil?

There is something I cannot understand at all. Why did the girls immediately recognise danger arriving with the men? Why did they know that they had to flee? What was the reason for their panic? Had there been something I don't know about that preceded this situation in the small cove? That must be the case.

It does not achieve anything to brainstorm about it. Willy-nilly, I will have to wait until tomorrow to clarify the situation. We could not go back now. We could not put our sailing boat and ourselves in danger for these girls, who — only perhaps — might be in danger. Maybe there's really a very simple explanation for everything. Maybe! Maybe I just overreacted, once again?

So, I will make the best of our situation and occupy myself some other way. A clean kitchen cloth lies spread over my lap and the dough bowl is standing on top of it. Now it is a matter of kneading the prepared mixture in the shallow bowl. Vigorously, I squeeze and beat the soft, warm dough with nimble hands, as though trying to kill a savage beast. Smack! Again and again, I press the soft mass into a flat circle, fold it together, slam the lump back into the bowl and knead it again. I love loose, fluffy bread; it just takes a bit of effort. My industrious hands are used to this work and do it nearly automatically, so that I can let my thoughts roam again. This time, they do not turn to the girls in danger, but to me and my skipper and partner, Alex.

For a year now, we have been living on this small sailboat and we have cruised the blue waters of the Caribbean. During this time, the small nutshell has become our cosy home and practical camper van — our world.

When I set foot on the sailboat for the first time and embarked on this journey with Alex, I knew nothing about boats, the sea, foreign countries, and also, nothing about the life surrounding all that. At first, I was astonished that it would be possible to live so rudimentarily, as I was a modern, technology-accustomed housewife with a convection oven, fully automatic washing machine and freezer. Collecting rainwater to drink, running five kilometres just to buy a kilogram of tomatoes, or preserving fruit juice with aspirin – I would never have dreamt of wanting to lead such a mundane life — or of being able to do it. But lo and behold, my fondness for Alex and the prospect of a wonderful trip quickly turned a demanding housewife into an adaptable, resourceful boat girl.

For me, it had been the proverbial leap into the dark.

And I'd been totally amazed. This strange world in which we are immersed has amazed and delighted me over and over again. I feel richly blessed.

Above all, the sea did it to me. At times, it is quiet and lovely, and calms you with its soft blue tones. At times, it frightens you with dangerous waves and hellish winds, and threatens you with danger and disaster. And then again, it is cold, leaden and heavy before us and keeps its secrets, good and bad, hidden in its unfathomable depths.

And boat life? From the very first day, it became my passion. So smoothly have I adapted to it, that it often seems to me that the boat has decided to take care of me and has adjusted to my whims.

It is a totally happy symbiosis.

Just like living together with Alex. Who would have thought that two people, who had accumulated as many idiosyncrasies and quirks over as many years as we had, could still adapt so readily to each other? Adapting to a situation of living in close confinement with each other, as we do in this tiny nutshell. Where you spend every day, every minute with each other, and share all experiences. Where you cannot dodge and keep out of each other's way, except in the allocation of work tasks. Alex is the skipper, responsible for the boat and navigation. I take care of all aspects of the household, supplies and shopping. So, each one of us has their scope of responsibility and does not interfere with the other.

And it has worked out well so far…well, mostly it works, I have to smile.

His special humour, his brown, loyal eyes and his now quite grey mop of curly hair have won me over. I especially love his way of making the most out of any situation, which is worth more than gold in this exotic world.

My wrists are starting to hurt. I stop, so that my weak arms can rest, but also to enjoy once again the fascinating panorama being offered all around me.

The backdrop of frayed palm trees, sitting on the white beach like a lace ruffle on the collar of a blouse, stands out impressively against the blue sky. This is reflected as an inverted image in the crystal clear waters of the small cove of Cay Caulker.

Now it occurs to me that I still need to marinate our fish for dinner tonight. My hands quickly shape the dough into two loaves. I put them both on a plate, side by side, cover them with the kitchen towel, and place it all so that it can absorb the sun in a sunny, sheltered spot on the seat cushions. The warm sun will then do its job.

I quickly climb down into the boat, and turning thoughts of the girls over in my head again and again, I remark to Alex, "Alex, the girls are very athletic, maybe they could have lost those men without much trouble."

"Why do you think that?"

"Do you remember when they were with us on the boat?"

"Hm...?" Two brown eyes look at me blankly.

"When we went swimming at the beach, we had to flop on the sand to rest. We were out of breath. The girls were there and Biene said to Kati sardonically, "Did they swim here direct from South America – the way they are wheezing?"

Alex now remembers, "Yes...we replied, only from the sailboat out there. But it was quite a few metres after all, plus we were no longer twenty and it was also hot."

I have to smile at this memory, "The girls were very surprised that we understood them. Biene turned red, as she was ashamed of her snide remark. She could not have known that someone in the middle of Central America would so easily understand her South German dialect."

"Sandra, you're digressing. What were you going to say?"

"Oh yeah...we had invited them to join us on the boat, to go swimming and to have a drink. So they could prove to us that they're more athletic than we are."

"But they weren't."

"But yes, Alex, they were..."

"They also had to wheeze quite a bit, but it's true, not as much as we did."

"I mean, they're pretty well trained. Surely, they were able to get away from those men."

"Sandra! It's no use, all of these "buts." We'll see tomorrow...," my wise Alex says once again.

We'll see tomorrow. Tomorrow! If only it weren't so long — until tomorrow.

Alex sits at the chart table. He has put the headphones over his ears and is listening to the local weather report. His forehead is wrinkled with sheer concentration, and I have to smile. Alex takes everything associated with the boat, with sailing and especially with the weather, incredibly seriously. Which, of course, is also perfectly fine with me. In the end, our safety depends on the fact that we subordinate ourselves at all times to the weather, because it is our ultimate boss. A strict boss that determines the choice of our sailing trips, travels, excursions, and anchorages.

"Is there bad weather coming our way?" I ask him.

I bend down close to him and press my cheek to his, with my ear next to his ear, and only the headphones in between. I want to hear too, but that is actually only an excuse, because I often just feel the need to be near him, to feel his skin and heat and to know — he is there.

Alex smiles at me, "It's whichever way you want to look at it. Perhaps it's not too bad. But quite a strong westerly wind is heading towards us around noon tomorrow. So, tomorrow morning we will return to Ambergris Cay, as agreed."

I twist one my unruly locks of hair into my hair clip and bend down even further to Alex. My cheek touches his smooth, brown shoulder, "Hmmm, tastes like salt and sun and…"

"Better stop, you witch, otherwise…"

I laugh into his face, "Otherwise what, my dear?"

Alex laughs mischievously and pulls my hair.

# Mysterious, the new neighbour

In the evening, the tranquillity of the quiet cove at Cay Caulker is over. A sleek motor-yacht moves majestically into the cove. Two tanned men work on the sails and set the anchor with loud shouts. The shouting and laughter also continues after they have anchored. Fortunately for us, the boat is quite a distance away, because music is now also getting turned up really loud.

Naturally, I get my binoculars. I have to see who has screwed up our peaceful evening.

A black-haired woman, she looks like a Latina, is dancing on the foredeck to South American music with lascivious, provocative movements. Her bikini top can barely restrain her two bulging spheres and her thong couldn't be a millimetre narrower. The lady has a great body and skin like velvet. Her wild, jet-black hair is dancing along with every move she makes. The two men, who have finished the anchoring manoeuvre, stand at the rail and watch the dancer.

Just now, a second young woman emerges from the cabin. She is the pure counterpart of her colleague. Her pale face is framed by fine blonde hair and her big blue eyes look around dreamily. Very delicate and pretty. She carries a tray full of glasses, bottles and cans to the table and puts it down carefully. Her movements are gentle and cautious. Now, she straightens up and binds her hair with a blue ribbon. For a moment, she stops and observes the Latina more carefully. Then she shakes her head and sits on the cockpit cushions with her back to the dancer. Strange, what you can read into the gestures even from a distance. Of course, I have to say that our binoculars, expensive things, are doing their best to provide some clarity.

A third young man brings out a plate with sandwiches from inside the boat, and puts it down on the bench. Now all of them sit down around the table and serve themselves.

Five people that come across very differently. The two young women are like Snow White and Rose Red. Their way of moving, gesticulating or eating is also totally different. The Latina chatters, waves her hands about, and in between, stuffs herself with food and drink. Snow-White sits there quietly, nibbling on a sandwich and sips on a glass — water, I suspect. She nods to any questions or shakes her head.

The blond young man next to her seems to be her brother. He is just as light-skinned and slender. He has the same small, finely chiselled face and the same calm manner. He also comes across as though he was having tea with a dear aunt and not on a boat in the Caribbean. He seems not quite at home in this crew.

The other three are behaving more loudly still. The shouting and laughter can easily be heard, even from where I am. The shrill voice of the Latina is mainly directed at the large, tanned man next to her. He has thick stubbly hair, an angular face and a resounding laugh. He is clearly American. I don't quite understand how you can identify that so well. Maybe it's his laugh? His haircut, or his clothes? Maybe it's just his mannerisms. In any case, he is bound to be American. And the Latina is his girlfriend.

The third young man, a strongly built, dark type, is trying to keep up with the gaiety of the other two. But, somehow, he seems to be the proverbial fifth wheel on the car. Again and again, he tries to address one of the others. Sometimes, he leans towards the blonde woman, where he meets with silence, or he says something to the Latina, where he is simply ignored. I can make out his frustration, even from this distance. Now he brings up fresh drinks, but the big guy, who's in charge on board, immediately has them returned with a vehement shake of his head. The Latina wants to seize yet another beer can, but a stern look from her boyfriend makes her stop.

The mood has changed.

They quickly finish eating and then, with a command, the skipper sends his people down inside the boat. Everyone comes back dressed in a shirt and boat shoes. Even the beautiful Latina has covered herself up with a sweater and jeans. What might they still be getting up to today?

Sighing, I sit down at the cockpit table. I had been expecting a cosy evening and had set out writing paper for a fax to my daughter Lisa; And now this.

Well, you can't always be lucky.

Alex sits down beside me and murmurs, "Just what we needed…"

"Can speak loudly, they're certainly not going to hear us."

But now the music is being turned down, as though they had understood us.

"What are they doing that for…?"

"American flag" I say, "young people, well, they certainly won't be staying long. It looks as if they're dressed for a night cruise."

I continue to watch our new neighbours. They are probably no longer all that young, the women in their thirties, the men about ten years older than that.

"Something's funny, Alex."

"Hm…"

"Why do you keep crouching at the rail and watching the island and the entrance to the cove? Nothing dangerous there, is there?"

"Ach, Sandra, you also crouch all the time with this thing in your hand."

Oh, how I hate these digs because of my binoculars and my interest in the environment and my fellow man.

"But I watch people and animals. I do not stare at the entrance to the cove, as if..."

"Perhaps they really want to leave soon and are preparing themselves?"

"No, no... They are just sitting there, excited. That looks strange to me."

"Strange, odd, dangerous...you're always seeing things!"

I continue as though Alex had not said anything, "The crew doesn't add up. The blond couple doesn't belong somehow."

"Maybe they're rich guests, who have booked a cruise in the Caribbean."

"Guests, who make sandwiches and serve drinks?"

Alex comments impatiently, "Oh Sandra, forget your snooping around and your famous intuition. Instead, get the bread out of the oven at long last. It smells wonderful."

The now fully baked bread gives off a really fantastic aroma and soon we are peacefully sitting around the table in the cockpit, spreading thick slices of bread with butter and eating fish to go with it. I mumble between two bites, "And I can bake fresh bread again tomorrow."

Regretfully, I look at the loaf of bread that is already very small.

"You've made two of them," Alex smiles, raising up his left eyebrow in his famous way and then says, "So fresh, it's simply the best."

"Ha, you don't know that at all. You give the poor bread no chance of getting a bit older!"

Alex changes the subject, "Tomorrow we must be up in time to be at Ambergris before the bad weather arrives..."

"And you know what we need to do there now!"

"Yeah, yeah...look for your disappeared girls. You're probably going to be highly embarrassed."

"Better to be embarrassed once too often, than..."

"Once?" my partner exclaims grimly, "Once..."

"Yes, my dear Alex, perhaps once or twice, but how many times have I been right with my..."

"Snooping around?" he mockingly asks.

"Intuition, and we were often able to help."

He snorts and shakes his head, eyes rolling.

I can't discuss things when he is in this mood. But at least he has promised to help me look for the girls tomorrow. So I now have to be patient.

Finally, I grab the paper already laid out, move to my corner of the cockpit and write a fax to my daughter Lisa. It is time to do that, anyway.

"Dear Lisa," I mutter, half aloud, "we are fine... "

"Don't make her envious of our beautiful life. Or, yes, do it, and then she may even come to visit us during her holidays."

Alex is sitting at the rail and letting his feet dangle. His ankle-length, printed cotton pants – Caribbean jeans, as I call them — suit him really well. Alex is remarkably tanned. His bare back looks as though it belongs to a Belizean. And his greying, short curly hair above it contrasts strongly.

"Holidays? That's exactly what I want to make attractive to her. I'll suggest that she comes here to Belize. Because it's beautiful, easy to reach by plane and we can sail to Belize City and pick her up."

Lost in thought, I gnaw at my pen, "I wonder if she'll come on her own or with George? If they're still together...?"

"Sandra! Why, for God's sake, shouldn't they still be together?"

"Oh Alex, I'm just always worried about my child and you know they have such totally different ideas about life."

"Oh, what are you thinking again? Why should it no longer be working between them all of a sudden? You're hearing the grass grow again. Everything's fine. She has her apartment, he has his. It's the best solution, anyway."

"Alex," I threateningly point my finger at him, "what is that supposed to mean again?"

It's just the way it is, that I take everything very personally.

"Well, maybe not for us, but you have to admit, your daughter is not exactly easy to handle."

"Ha," I cry out, "but are you...or am I?

We look at each other and we have to laugh. We know that each of us has his "grind" and opinions, quirks and habits, which have become ingrained over many years. It is likely that, as we have grown older, we have hardened positions in our views and opinions. But because we love each other, we want to live together, and therefore also find a compromise in nearly every point at issue. Or one or the other, at times me or at times Alex, takes the edge off somewhat, and meets the other one more than half way.

There is only one habit that we have not yet ground down at all.

Alex has a devilish habit of looking at all pretty women. And I am extremely jealous. But there are simply too many beautiful women in the Caribbean.

"Admiring natural beauty" is what Alex calls it, and he says that I am just a jealous woman and take everything too personally.

But I feel that it really is an affront to me personally, when he flirts with these women. Particularly, when I am left to feel that I am the "old" one, standing by stupidly.

Let's see whether we ever succeed in removing these issues.

"And you, Sandra, do you really think Lisa will come here? She has already promised it so often."

My thoughts return to the fax, "Yes, why not, let's see."

Eagerly, I continue to write a whole page.

Just as I fold up the paper, I notice there, on the back, a drawing scribbled half in my subconscious; A sketch of a boat. Amazed, I notice that I've recorded our new neighbour, the motor-yacht, on paper. And pretty much exactly so, in terms of the construction, the sailing mast, the flag and the name "Amigo."

So now I'm doing things without being aware of doing them...maybe I'm growing old? But being only close to fifty, hopefully not senile yet!

Now, in addition to the sketch of the boat, I start to draw the people.

The dancing Latina in the skimpy thong; the delicate blonde, fair-skinned, beautiful lady; the beefy, sourpuss man at the rail, and the blond, soft-skinned fellow who could be the brother of the gentle lady.

And lastly, the sporty skipper barking out commands, with his tanned skin, blond, short-cut hair and his noisy manner. An American, and the owner of the racy boat?

Are the others his crew? Or guests, as Alex says?

Charter guests who have come to this beautiful cove in Belize on vacation? They don't swim or dive, they don't go snorkelling, despite the fact that Cay Caulker is known for its beautiful coral.

They don't go to the beach for a walk.

People on a Caribbean vacation?

Alex comes into the cockpit with two drinks in his hands, "You're still busy with those people?"

"Well, if you ask me, Alex, there is something not right at all with those people over there."

"I am not asking you and also I don't want to know about it. Cheers!"

# Dangerous trip to the beach

Startled, I sit up and stiffly squat in bed. My ears are pricked and my alarm antennas have extended.

Is there something scratching on our boat? It sounds so close.

There, again this scraping noise. Ice shivers run down my spine.

Everything I can imagine as a possible origin for these sounds goes through my head and is filtered by: "explicable," "harmless" and "dangerous."

I look at Alex, who blissfully keeps on sleeping. His oddly crooked face stays relaxed and peaceful. He has heard nothing.

There it is again, this scratching and rattling sound. I claw my fingers on the hatch and stare outside. At first, I can't see anything. Then I look over to the "Amigo" between the fishing boats. In the weak reflection of one of its onboard lamps, I see a small motorboat moored alongside. Just barely, I can make out figures, who heave some packages from this small boat onto the deck of the "Amigo."

So not onto our boat! Uff…

But still far too close…and in the middle of the night! In a secluded cove? What are they doing that is forbidden? So secretly?

Don't they mind the closeness of our sailing boat? Or did they simply not notice it, here between the fishing boats? After all, our boat is a little distance away, on the northern edge of the small cove.

Scratching. Rumbling.

Now, however, I must check what is mysteriously going on.

They would not have vegetables and meat delivered in the middle of the night?

Should I wake up Alex? Not a good idea, because I need to remain here, keep still and thoroughly think about matters first.

"Lies start you running," he always tells me. That is a rule that you instil in little children so they don't run across the street. And what he wants to tell me with the saying from kindergarten times, 'Look, Listen, Go,' is that I always start running too fast, without thinking very much beforehand.

Is that now also the case? Of course not. Because if I think too long, perhaps a good opportunity to discover something will be lost.

Sure, I must be careful, and make sure they do not see me, because if things are a bit fishy, they will certainly not want someone sticking their nose into it.

Alex is still asleep. Now it occurs to me that he put plugs into his ears before falling asleep. Sometimes, if he expects it to be a loud night, he does that as a precautionary measure. Aha, that's why he didn't hear a thing. Alright, let him sleep on.

Carefully, I climb out of bed and sneak into the saloon. While going out, I grab my clothes and slip into a top and shorts. It is sufficient for a tropical night.

Cautiously, I scurry into the cockpit and peep over the bench cushion.

Immediately, the noise reaches me more clearly.

No music, no laughter and no fun or holiday noise is to be heard at all, but the subdued sliding and pushing of something on the deck.

My eyes must first get accustomed to the darkness, but slowly, different things peel out from the night.

The small motorboat still lies alongside and two men lift out crates that are then taken onto the "Amigo" by active shadowy figures. Now, the small boat is cast off, the engine howls and it disappears around the corner of the island.

But a second small boat already circles into the cove and sets course for the American motor-yacht.

I am simply much too far away to be able to see them properly. And the fishing boats between us obstruct my view. The "Amigo" lies in the centre of the cove. And that's exactly where I should be. Or at least as close as possible.

In the saloon, I set our radio to receive, get our small camera and the walkie-talkies, pack both into double plastic bags, and I am already on the way up again and standing at the rail. I clamp the plastic bag holding the devices between my teeth and carefully, without making a noise, I slip down the side of the boat into the warm water. With slow arm and leg movements, I circle round the fishing boats that give me good cover all the way to the shore. I crawl from the water behind a few shrubs and hurry on, hunched over. My path leads me up to the edge of the sandy area in the shade of some beach spruces. So, I circle half the cove in their protection. Crouching low, now I run over the beach to the shore. I get cover behind a few smaller coral rocks that rise up sharp and black from the sand.

Just now, a pale moon peeps out from between some clouds and I stare at my pale legs and arms. Despite my long stay in the Caribbean, I cannot yet be regarded as a Belizean. Also my grey-white hair betrays me. Quickly, I spread a handful of greyish sand mud over my limbs, neck, and face. I make my long hair slick with mud and stick it closely together on my head.

Who knows, maybe this is one of these healthy mud packs.

However, now I have different concerns than the health of my skin and hair.

The camera is quickly released from the plastic and is ready to take pictures. I wonder whether the night with the waning moon is bright enough to be able to take pictures without flash. I simply have to try. Flash…that would give me away immediately. My trembling fingers find the flash off button and I duck into position.

Fear, what are you doing here? Trembling fingers, calm down. Heartbeat, let up. No-one can work like that!

Carefully, I peek the lens over the rocks, snapping pictures of the object of my interest, two, three times, and then crawl back. My heart races, my skin is sweaty.

Fearfully, I wait for any reaction. Then I carefully look over the rocks again.

The men are still working away. Their movements are hectic. They probably haven't noticed me.

But wait! One of the women is standing at the bow of the "Amigo." Judging by her curves, it is the black haired Latina and — yes — she is looking around with binoculars. Dammed! I was not paying attention very well.

I now have to retreat. But where to? I can't leave the beach and hide amongst the palm trees. It's much too far. It's also not possible to swim off. They would be able to detect my movements far too well.

I am just wondering what strategy I should choose, when once again, a small motor boat drives into the cove, lines up alongside the "Amigo" and behold, these men also start to heave crates onto the yacht. The Latina runs to the stern of the boat and while the rest of the crew are distracted, I dare to take another picture.

Maybe one too many, because the Latina must have noticed something. She turns in my direction. In the meantime, it has become a touch lighter. She calls a few words and points towards the shore.

I suddenly go hot and cold. I duck down deep between the rocks, wrap the camera in a plastic bag, put the package in a rock hole and seal it with a stone. If *I'm* found, they shouldn't get the photos.

My next cautious peek over the rocks almost causes my heart to stop. Between the palm tree trunks, three men step out, black as the night and all with shoulders at least as broad as boxer Ali in his best times. Two clearly wear a police uniform. Police officers? Why am I seeing policemen everywhere?

Policemen, who pursue girls? And policemen who hang around on a mysterious motor-yacht, a boat with strange people on it, who load odd crates in the middle of the night?

Why do I have the uncomfortable feeling that I cannot get any help from these police officers? Why am I not persuaded to put myself under their protection?

What can I do now?

As soon as I notice that the three men are concentrating on the motor-yacht, and the Latina is getting the dinghy ready, I try to retreat. But it's not working. The policemen march across the beach and look around. It won't be much longer before they find me in an anxious heap behind the rocks. But suddenly, they turn round and walk towards the dinghy, which has almost reached the shore.

Phew, what luck. But I still can't feel safe, I must urgently see how to get away from here.

Just now, the men reach the dinghy and are joking with the young beauty. Totally distracted, and because their dinghy engine is running, they cannot hear me.

My last resort is the walkie-talkie. Alex has to help me now.

Turn it on, tune to our channel, call out to him in a whisper...Yes, that can be done.

"Alex, Alex, Alex."

I pray, whisper, call.

"Alex, Alex, Alex."

And finally a crackle:

"Where? Why?"

"Listen – JUST LISTEN – south end of the cove, a small group of rocks, come with the dinghy, quick."

Immediately I turn off the radio again; it crackles and rattles much too loudly.

The men are discussing things with the woman. I'm just considering whether I should photograph that as well, when they leave the shore and move quickly to the centre of the island. So, no photograph.

Yet again they are far too close to my rocks. I press myself into the sand a little deeper and pretend to have fainted — perhaps been mugged? — as a last resort, should they come and find me.

I duck closely into the rocks and wait, trembling with fear, until the men have crossed the beach, reach the palm trees and disappear between the tree trunks. But are they really gone? I don't dare to rely on it.

The Latina returns to the "Amigo." Now, the last of the small boats leaves the "Amigo." The crew on the luxury yacht quickly and remarkably quietly clean up the boat, handle the sails, raise the anchor and move out of the cove.

Lucked out again.

My forehead is wet with sweat and my hands are trembling. I take a deep breath. My recklessly hasty adventure could have ended terribly.

A good ten minutes pass again for sure, and then I hear a noise that sounds like music to my ears.

Our dinghy, the most wished-for tender. From the water, my rescue approaches in the form of an inflatable boat and a surely mad-as-hell Alex, who is bound to tear me into a hundred shreds.

Maybe the police would have been the lesser of two evils?

Quickly, I get the camera from the hole, pack it into the plastic bag together with the walkie-talkie and wedge everything under my top. Behind the rocks, I dip into the water, washing the mud from my hair, and pull myself into the dinghy — without the help of an available gentleman.

My skipper, partner and lifesaver drives silently, with tight mouth, to our sailboat.

My goodness, how can those beautifully curved lips look so angry? So hard? How can these admired, tanned shoulders remain so rigid? Have such a rejecting effect?

Once we arrive on the boat, Alex silently barricades himself in the cabin, turns on the radar at the navigation table and pulls out the appropriate nautical charts, in order to find an escape route in case of an emergency, should someone have noticed something. He studies a possible course to Belize City that we could handle even when visibility is poor. Then he switches the radio over to the emergency call channel.

"It would not do any good calling the police, Alex, as they were actually already in place. On the beach, two police officers were clearly there, and were discussing things with the woman from the American boat."

Without a word to his boat girl — for example, *Did you see anything else? Was it bad?* — This block of wood lies down on the bed dressed just as he is, turns over and starts to snore loudly.

Maybe he really has already fallen asleep, as it was a tiring night for him too, but a quick *"Hi, how are you?"* would not really have hurt.

# And what about those crates now?

In spite my frayed nerves, I manage to doze off briefly, but I do not sleep deeply. Then, I sense that Alex is lying awake and is tossing back and forth nervously. Our bunk is not very wide and the continuous mattress passes on the effects of turning and bouncing to the other adjacent person. Usually, my dear Alex complains continuously that I sleep jerkily and move to and fro terribly, but it's now him for a change.

I notice now that he gets up from our camp, flips open his chart table in the saloon and rummages around in the pile of sea charts. What is my good skipper looking for in the sea charts in the middle of the night?

I stagger sleepily into the saloon and rub my tired eyes. Alex is standing at the saloon table with a chart spread out in front of him, and he is studying it with his index finger moving around on it.

"Come here and help me."

"At one-thirty in the morning? You're beyond help!" I turn around and want to crawl back into my warm bed.

"Come on, Sandra, it's important!"

"In the middle of the night," I grumble, but obediently, I sit down next to him.

"Try to remember exactly your visit to the police the day before yesterday…"

"Yes, what about it?"

Alex looks at me searchingly.

With enormous effort, I try to bring my brain cells into action, which does not happen very quickly, considering the sleepy night hour. "The day before yesterday?"

"Yes."

"I remember that as soon as we had arrived at Ambergris Cay, yes, it was the day before yesterday, I wanted to buy fruit in the village. Did you mean that?"

"Yes, and I had asked you…"

"…Asked me to inquire at the police station, whether the upper entrance to the neighbouring island was still closed off for sailing boats. Which, as it turned out, was no longer the case."

"Yes, and then…what did you tell me had exactly happened at the police station?"

"Aha, yes there was a lot going on. The office was full of smoke. Many men, policemen also, were puffing away like crazy. They were excited, loudly discussed things and were waving their arms around. Again and again, I heard words like 'drifting, been lost, current, crate, disaster' and such things."

Thinking intensely, I try to remember exactly what I had heard. But my English! And still then this Belizean gibberish! And I was standing at the door, almost still outside, somewhat hidden by a shelf with police paraphernalia. So I couldn't understand everything that well.

"It was clearly about something that had happened somewhere and that something important or valuable was lost. Everyone was screaming at once…"

Now, something emerges from the unfathomable depths of my subconscious mind. An image of the smoky office, the heat, many men; most of them black, a few Latinos and a white man.

"And there was this quiet man sitting on the chair near the door. Also a black man, with thick curly hair and round, sad eyes. He started to speak softly. Something about full moon and tide. I understood "High Tide." Again, about crates and Ambergris Cay, from the South, about...yes, about a shark and a reef, where no boat would get in, but a crate. "Speak up, Ashton!" a police officer had called out and all the others fell silent as a mouse. But since the quiet man, Ashton, then said the same thing again, not anything that concerned me, I thought I could quickly go shopping and return here later. Which is what I then did."

Alex looks at me again, pondering. He's just my dear, smart Alex. What I find out with my instinct, he explores with reason and makes a logical connection. He now says, namely, "Ambergris Cay, the south, full moon and high tide…"

Confused, I look at my skipper, but he pulls me closer to the table and points to the chart. I see Ambergris Cay, the lagoon before it, the reef that bounds it on the eastern side and a few smaller islands all around. "Yes, and?" I ask.

Alex moves his finger across the chart, speaking slowly and clearly, "Ambergris, south, reef, this reef here is Shark Reef…and look at this cove behind this reef!"

I feel quite weird, because all of a sudden a light goes on, despite it being the dead of night.

"Alex, that's…that's the small cove, the cove where we…" I have to sit down.

A grim nod from Alex, "Exactly. A valuable crate gets lost there, and somehow it floats through the reef at high tide and lands on the beach…"

"The men found out from the quiet man the day before yesterday that the crate must be there, searched for it yesterday and…" I get ever quieter, "… found the crate and the girls. My goodness, Alex, that is…the...that must..." My shaky voice stops.

"Drugs! Heroin, or something like it."

"Of course the men chased the girls, and we can't go to the police, because..."

"...One of them was involved."

"And," Alex tops that, "beside us was a luxury motor-yacht, onto which crates were loaded at night...!"

Now I am really nauseous!

"Do you still remember what the fisherman of Placencia told us? What was his name ... Paul? The one who showed us how to catch crayfish?"

"I remember vaguely. Oh, yes, of course. He said a colleague of his had found such a crate. He told us that the American drug investigators, who help the police in Belize to find the drug boats, were roaming along the whole coast and had broken up many of those criminal rings."

"And that when a police boat comes near to them," Alex continues, "these criminals throw the drugs overboard, where they are collected by small motor boats and returned to the drug boats. Drugs packed in plastic pouches and crates."

"And, Alex," I ask sheepishly, "didn't the fishermen from Placencia also say... his colleague, who had found such a crate and wanted to keep it, had died under mysterious circumstances?"

"Died, yes...but not under mysterious circumstances. He clearly said that his friend had been weighed down with stones...and drowned. It was clearly a punishment from these criminals."

Alex makes a decision, "We must try to reach the police in the capital city of Belmopan. We must not expose ourselves, and above all, we must protect ourselves."

"Shouldn't we go to the police in Belize City now?"

"And then reveal that we have seen something? And what tells us that the police there are not also...?"

"Yes,...the same region, perhaps the same people."

"We must continue as normal. Tomorrow, we will return to Ambergris, look for the girls and then see what happens."

"Do you think we'll be safe at Ambergris?"

"Safer than here, in any case. Among tourists at the resort."

"Do you think that they noticed anything?" I ask sheepishly.

"That you were there on the shore? Certainly not. I am convinced that you…we would no longer be alive if they had."

Great thought! But maybe I really had been lucky once again.

We try to sleep a little, but with these worries and fears, no sleep can be expected to come, of course.

# Naturally this must be followed up!

As soon as Alex has prepared everything for the trip to Ambergris, he has nothing better to do than to reproach me. He can understand, he says, that I'm worried about the girls — he is too — but from now on, I should really stop embarking on such dangerous trips, like last night...

"But..."

"No buts, Sandra!"

"But..."

"No, are you actually aware of how much danger you've just managed to escape from? What do you think these drug pushers would have done to you?"

"I know that, but otherwise, how would we have found all this out? And..."

"We could have found out about it without your dangerous adventure."

"But I even have proof. The photos!"

"You still don't know what you managed to get on camera! With only a little moonlight and without flash."

"I should have used flash?"

I should have done nothing at all, Alex says now. And, should I do something like that again, then, then...My dear Alex scolds and threatens me and wishes for all the devils to get at my throat.

Until I can't take it any longer and escape into the bathroom.

In the bathroom, I wash my sleepy eyes and look in the mirror.

What? What are you telling me, my trusty blue eyes?

We have seen the girls in a panic. We have seen the men pursuing them, one was in uniform, and we have observed strange happenings at night on the motor-yacht. And again, two men in uniform!

So, and you are not mistaken?

The blue eyes smile at me, no, no, we are not mistaken.

And don't you also have the urge, no, the obligation, to help the girls? Will you refrain from observing and spying in future?

No, we will not!

"Ha," I say to my mirror image, "I won't either"

"What did you say?" Alex calls out from the saloon.

"When are we going to sail to Ambergris?"

"As soon as we're ready and the boat's ready."

He examines the sky. He had already heard the weather forecasts, "It's OK, as far as I'm concerned."

Slowly, we leave our anchorage, where we spent the night.

The peaceful cove at Cay Caulker is now blank and innocent in the early morning sunshine.

# Initial investigations at the holiday resort

The wind has freshened somewhat and this has given us a rapid sailing trip. But anyway, since I wanted to look for the girls as quickly as possible, this has been just right for me.

We have made the passage from Cay Caulker to Ambergris Cay in record time. As soon as we have threaded our way into the reef entrance, the wind dies down completely.

Once Alex has sunk our anchor in the sand, we pack a few things and go to the resort by dinghy. Alex leaves me at a small table beside the pool and says he wants to go to Hal Morgan, the Hotel Manager, and check on the girls — alone.

"I would also like to come along…"

"No, I want to go alone, simply to check out the situation, without a lot of turmoil…"

"Aha, you think I create turmoil!"

"…And then I'll come and get you."

"But don't say anything about the American boat and thus …"

"…Promised. First I want to see what's up with the girls… and you, you…"

"Yes, I'll…" I sigh devotedly.

"What will you do? Say it loudly and clearly. I want to hear it."

"I'll stay here and do nothing."

"Hm…"

"Anyway, I'm too tired to…"

So now I'm really dead tired and I squat in one of these stupid combinations, ornamental small table and little chair, that is anything but comfortable. The wobbly table top does not even have enough stability to lean an elbow on. And I have such a heavy head, for which I'd love to have some support.

Mary, one of the amiable employees of the resort, brings me a colourful fruit juice. She looks sad and her lips that are usually split wide in laughter, scarcely divide into a quiet "Morning." Mary looks pretty in her black skirt, which is the hotel uniform, together with her white blouse. With her mint-coloured bandana, the outfit looks a little happier than I can say about Mary herself. In low spirits, she looks at me.

Shyly, she glides her nervous hands over the small table, as though she had discovered a few crumbs. Her face betrays her readiness to give me information about something that I have actually already known for a long time. But I would not like to pre-empt Alex. Above all, I want him to have to report to me himself that the girls have disappeared. That I was right.

My God, Sandra, you are petty!

Mary looks at me again with dark, questioning eyes. Then she turns round and disappears into the restaurant.

Alex told me that I should stay here, which I promised to him. I am surprised at myself…that I am so obedient. But I have really overdone it a bit in the last few days with my spying, and so now I want to wait. I will still give him another five minutes.

I suck on my fruit juice and wonder.

When I'm pinned down here, it doesn't mean that I can't open my eyes and ears and that my brain shouldn't turn on.

With my eyes swollen to slots because of the sleepless night, I squint into the sun and take a look around.

My eyes roam over the glittering turquoise pool, the colourful flowers of the carefully manicured grounds, between the tall palm trees to the beach and also out to sea, shimmering in all shades of green and blue. I sigh, this is a soothing sight. Isn't this a beautiful, wonderful world?

But, hold it! There's something very wrong here. Shouldn't children be frolicking around, shouldn't adults be swimming and snorkelling, shouldn't young people be competing with each other on the volleyball field?

Why isn't there anyone in the water? And anyone sitting at any of the small tables, like I am sitting at mine?

I am all alone. There is no-one to be seen, far and wide. That is confirmation for me that something is wrong at the resort, that something terrible must have happened to the girls.

I now notice a young woman, who comes over to me from the restaurant. It is Sandy, the attractive tour guide, a Creole from Martinique, whom I met a few days ago through the two girls, Katharina and Sabine. Sandy squats down at my small table, eyes red from crying, "It's terrible…terrible…mon Dieu."

"Sandy, what in heaven's name has happened?"

"They are gone, simply disappeared…" Sandy blows her nose and starts to talk, and in her excitement, she does so in her Martinique French. Since I understand that better than the Belizean English, that is quite alright with me.

"Et bien! I was very upset last night," she reported. "It really isn't okay to stay out that long. These young girls are absolutely inconsiderate. They probably hung out in a disco, not in the least thinking that anyone here was worried about them. On the day before, when the girls told me of their plans, I was happy about this personal initiative, but explicitly impressed on them to be sure to be back at nightfall. The girls had promised me that: of course they were going to be there, at about six o'clock, they would have to return the boat again anyway. "

Sandy is now looking at me desperately, "It got ever later and then, it was suddenly pitch-black night. And not the slightest trace of Kati and Biene.

Duky, the bartender, came up to me, because he had noticed that something was wrong. I was running around everywhere, asking about the girls. Sandy goes on to explain, "Duky asked whether something had happened, if he could do anything to help. Nice as can be, he offered to help me, but then laughed when he heard what the problem was. "These are young girls…Girls, they like fun. They will be out somewhere, dancing and having a party, and you're getting worried.""

Sandy is crying again, "That's what I also thought at first, but…" she now says hesitantly. "But the two of them had gone off in shorts and shirts, I can't imagine that they would go to a disco dressed like that. Or to a party!"

Sandy, the tour guide, shakes her head. She believes that the girls would have come back, albeit for just a second, to change or at least to touch up their makeup.

"Maybe they did and no one noticed them?" I interject cautiously.

"No, no, I was in their room. It was still all tidied up, as the chambermaid had left it in the morning. Have you ever seen a bathroom and bedroom after two girls have prettied themselves up in it for the evening?"

I have to smile, despite myself, and Sandy continues, "Duky sent the boy to the boat rental shop, in order to see whether they had returned the boat — and then he wanted to see where to go from there."

"Twenty minutes later," Sandy continues her tale, "the boy returned from the boat hire and reported that the operator was furious, because he would have gladly ended his workday a long time ago, but the young ladies were still not back with his boat. The girls had promised him they would be there at six in the evening. He had even threatened them that they would have to pay ten dollars for each overtime hour. He always handled his rentals in such a way, as he knows how they are, the young ones. The boy reported that the rental operator told him that the girls had set off in a southerly direction. On his advice, because the most beautiful bays and coral reefs were within easy reach there."

Immediately, I see the small bay before my mind's eye. That tiny, beautiful — and yet so dangerous bay.

"I was shocked," Sandy says, "but Duky tried to comfort me, "it does not have to mean that something is wrong," he said. But he was now also in favour of going to inform the hotel manager."

Sandy broods about what happened, then she continues to elaborate, "He, I mean Hal Morgan, the manager, suggested first asking around among the staff and guests. This is what we then did, all three of us. Hal Morgan went around the hotel, and asked the women in the kitchen. Duky went from room to room in the accommodations of the employees and I," says Sandy, "took advantage of a short break between two dance performances in the grand hall and seized the microphone. I explained to the guests that the two girls had not yet returned from a boat trip and that I was worried about this, and that I would like to ask each of those present to think about whether they had seen the girls at some point today, especially in the evening, be it in the hotel or on the premises. The people looked at each other, considering my words, and then began, one after the other, to shake their heads or mumble something negative. I returned to the hotel lobby, where Duky, Hal Morgan and a few people from the staff stood together. Hal Morgan divided people into groups and instructed them to make rounds through the resort, then to meet up back here again and, hopefully, to bring the girls along. Very carefully, the instructions were implemented and the girls would have definitely been found, if they had been somewhere on site. But unfortunately, all of them returned without Kati and Biene."

Sandy blows her nose violently and dabs her handkerchief over her eyes, "I..." she sobs, "I do have the responsibility for these children."

As much as possible, I try to comfort the tour guide. But I am upset myself, because I know where and how I had last seen the girls. That's something I can't tell Sandy, because it's something I only want to tell the state police. Hopefully, Alex will also stick to this agreement, because what we had seen there in the small bay should not be reaching the wrong ears. And now that we know that Kati and Biene have disappeared, our observations have a much larger and more dangerous significance.

"Come on, Sandy, let's go and join the others."

But now Duky, the bartender, turns round the corner and comes towards us. He is an attractive man, with his coffee-brown skin, typical of those of Euro-African ethnicity, and his almond-shaped eyes, which also suggest an Indian in the long line of his African and European ancestry. He looks like a carved, ebony sculpture. His hair is shaved off totally on the sides and only right at the top of his head, a thick strip of dreadlocks is growing steeply upright like a punk's. They bob along with every step he takes. On his left ear, a tiny, silver monkey earring has been clamped, and the monkey looks like it wants to perform exercises there. Now, however, Duky's face is somewhat greyish and the usually bright eyes look dull and sad.

"Biene and Kati had told me of their plans," he starts to report, "that they wanted to set out in a rental boat for the southern bays. No problem – I encouraged them. Ambergris Cay is safe and the town of "San Pedro" is a really cool place. Only, they would have to be back just before dark, I demanded...and they must stay away from the cottage settlement. No place for young ladies. And I wished them a lot of fun — hi man, I didn't know that..."

His utterance trails off into a murmur, and then he is gone, around the next corner.

Now, Alex hurries towards me from the restaurant. He sees Sandy sitting with me, "Aha, you already know."

"She came of her own accord, I haven't..."

"Okay, now come on."

He takes me by the arm and leads me to the dining room. And here, I see all the people that I've missed out in the pool and on the beach.

"Aha, everybody is here... only I had..."

"Don't complain now, Sandra. As I see it, you haven't wasted time."

The mood in the dining hall is very depressed. Where laughter and chitchat is usually heard always be heard, one now hears muffled voices and inconclusive murmurings.

Hal Morgan stands up in front of the people. His face is grey and dead serious. His familiar, broad American smile has disappeared, and with subdued words, he explains, "As you have now learned, two of our guests, the two German girls, Sabine and Katharina, disappeared yesterday. They made a trip with a small rental boat and did not return. We do not know anything about their disappearance, we have no idea what happened. The police have been informed and are taking care of the matter..." He looks into the faces of his guests and continues, "... the sad disappearance of the two girls is something we are terribly sorry about — just like all of you. We hope very much that the two girls will soon emerge healthy and happy again. We have a capable, enormously committed police force and the girls are going to be found soon."

The "a capable police force" sends a shiver down my spine and I turn to face Alex.

There is no significant reaction. His stony face shows me, however, that he is also not comfortable with this, but he simply has himself more under control.

A short pause, and now Hal Morgan's voice sounds encouraging, "We don't want fearful assumptions, or an anxious wait for news, to overshadow your holiday. It isn't useful either to the issue itself, or to the two girls, if everybody hangs around here, waiting for news and foregoes all those distractions which make the wait a little easier. I propose, therefore, that you pursue all your activities as usual and I promise you that we will tell you immediately, as soon as we know something. We are in touch with the dive boats and tour buses on the radio and they can come back at any time and celebrate with the girls their happy return, which we all hope for."

Then he wishes everyone a relaxing day.

The people are actually all starting to get up, and reluctantly, they start to go outside, to disperse to the boats, to stroll by the pool or on the beach.

Hal Morgan holds a similar speech for the employees, whom he has ordered into the dining room, only that the words "Distraction" and "Tour" are replaced by "Work." So, life at the hotel begins to normalize again a bit.

Alex and I, at last, sit alone in the dining room.

"Alex, what are we going to do?"

He shrugs his shoulders helplessly. Helplessly? My clever Alex, who always has good ideas. Ideas that do not arise from intuition or hunches like mine, but are well founded and rational.

"Think about it a bit."

I freshen up in the hotel's washroom. That is, I cool down my overheated neck, my hot face, and I run cold water over my wrists. Searchingly, I look into my own pale face.

You were right, my blue eyes. And everything was seen correctly, there in the small bay.

Two blue eyes look back at me in sorrow, today neither smiling nor radiant, only infinitely sad and despondent.

I feel the same way. Exactly the same, I nod to them and return to Alex.

We speak to many people, but learn nothing new. So, we go for a swim and have lunch at the exquisite buffet that leaves no culinary wishes. But, somehow, I'm not really all that hungry.

We pass the afternoon swimming and lazing about, and in the evening, we sit together again with Hal Morgan. The American looks even sadder than he had in the morning. His loud, cheerful, optimistic character got lost somewhere between yesterday and today. He runs his hand through his hair nervously and I feel sorry for him.

"The village police still haven't found or learned anything?"

"No", he replies, distressed, "no sign of the girls, no message from a kidnapper..."

"Where are the police searching?"

Hal gives me a funny look and shrugs his shoulders, "They do not tell me what they are doing, of course, but...I guess they are doing their job."

It was not overly confident, the way this came out of his mouth. Maybe he also suspects something? But Alex and I see that it is useless to ask any further questions. Hal leaves us and we remain behind, somewhat helpless.

Alex frowns and is just as confused as I am. "I don't know, a little bit more...concern...for the girls is what I would have wished for..."

"Hal looked really concerned."

"That...yes. But he hardly asks questions, wouldn't he have to..."

"Perhaps he is a good friend of the police chief."

"Sandra, no suspicions, please. But you're right, it's all so vague, so indefinite. No one's searching properly, nobody is investigating. I also don't know what to say."

My Alex, who otherwise always knows what is going on, is always looking for a solution and always finds a way out!

So I say, "Hm, I...I think we should go to our boat and consider what more can be done."

"A sensible idea, and Hal will surely inform us, if there's any news. "

Silently, we leave the resort and return to the *Seeschwalbe* by dinghy. It's getting late, and I quickly make us a bite to eat and we sit down in the living room with a glass of wine.

Still helpless.

Alex's bushy eyebrows are drawn together, his lips are pressed tight into a thin line and his face has a greyish tint. A bleak picture.

I think that my face probably looks about the same.

After a long consideration, I begin, "May I suggest something?"

His approving gaze makes me continue, "How about we leave the mooring tomorrow and sail along outside the reef towards the South. We look very carefully whether we can discover any sign of the girls, anything, at the reef, among the corals, or on the shore of Ambergris. A piece of garment, the wooden boat, anything. Then we return here…"

"…and if, by then, the girls are still not there, I will personally call the state police in the capital city of Belmopan!"

Without discussing much more, we prepare the sailing boat for tomorrow's search operation and go to bed early.

The certainty that Alex believes me and will help me in the search makes for a restful, profound sleep.

The best part is that Alex lays his tanned arm around my shoulder, and squeezes it in his sleep a couple of times…an extremely pleasant feeling.

# Search operation on the reef

It is still almost completely dark, but Alex and I are already awake. We clearly slept too little, both of us, but...ah well. We still cannot sail off. With all the reefs, shoals and coral gardens, which are ponderously wedged between our mooring point and the open sea, it would be far too dangerous in this darkness. In order to see the dangers, we need good sunlight. So, I first prepare a rich breakfast and lay the small table in the cockpit. Thoughtfully, we drink the fruit juice, eat the three-minute eggs and chew rather listlessly on the bread and marmalade. Neither of us has much of an appetite. But since we don't know when we will have time to eat again during the next few hours, we eat a certain amount of calories and vitamins. Thus, we will get through the day without breaking down.

The rising sun gives us the signal to leave.

Hastily, I clear the table, wash the dishes and tuck them into the boxes provided for this purpose. While I close all the hatches and take the sailing equipment into the cockpit, Alex begins to pull up the anchor.

The "Seeschwalbe" is on her way through the lagoon. I am at the wheel and try to assess whether the light is already sufficient to detect enough in the water. Slowly, I steer the boat in the direction of the passage.

The sun is already high enough to clearly show us the reef edge through the water and the dark-blue cut-off to the deeper water.

Alex now takes over the wheel, and I stand at the bow and give him hand signals. So, we manoeuvre carefully and slowly through the passage and out into the open sea. Since the reef drops steeply on the seaward side, we can manoeuvre fairly close along it. The course southward is quickly set. The sea is absolutely calm today. There are no waves to break the smooth surface, and so, we can clearly see the protruding edges of the reef, the corals and even the fish in the clear water. Because there is too little wind for sailing and we can also navigate much closer along the reef by using the engine, we leave the sails rolled up. Alex concentrates on navigation and I squat on the rail and observe the area with binoculars. I am trying to identify anything, especially on the reef plate, that could be human or belong to a person, such as clothing, fins or similar; anything that can easily get stuck on the jagged coral edges. Then I swivel the binoculars towards the sea and look across the water. The surface extends in front of me, blue and shiny. I cannot see the slightest interruption or defect in this endless, absolutely flat expanse. Only a few seagulls draw their usual circles, shouting hoarse messages into the clear air and diving into the water from time to time, in order to snatch up one of the silvery fish, of which hundreds are shooting back and forth through the water.

Now, I turn the binoculars back towards the coast again and look carefully at the beaches of the Ambergris peninsula, where I hope to find the small boat. The bays had already been searched by the employees of the hotel, but how far towards the South have they extended their search?

Anyway, no one knows where the police have searched.

So, checking every stretch of beach thoroughly, I'm trying to make something out in the shade of the palm trees that doesn't belong there and search through the clear waters of the lagoon with my eagle eyes. In particular, we thoroughly examine the small bay, which we recognize immediately. Alex throttles the engine, so we move slowly past. Nothing!

We soon reach the southern tip of Ambergris peninsula.

Silently, we continue, with Alex at the wheel and me on the rail with the binoculars. Only now, as we move past the southernmost point of Ambergris and another bit beyond it, we make a big turn to port and steer a little away from the reef, back towards the North.

We have already been on the move for over three hours now, and we have only covered about ten miles at this slow pace. I remain sitting on the same side of the boat and can search the open sea more thoroughly this time. A few dolphins accompany the *Seeschwalbe* a good part of the way. They eye me curiously, heads held diagonally, and then disappear into the open sea — once there is nothing new to discover anymore about this amusing, large fish that our boat must represent to them. As though neatly lined up, a group of pelicans moves past the boat slowly, without taking even the slightest notice of us. Fast, white sea gulls are begging for fish waste with high-pitched screams, and these too soon leave the unproductive place behind again.

"You're right, I, too, am hungry," I call after them. Quickly, I slip down into the boat cabin, cut a few slices of bread and cold roast on a cutting board, set out two cans of Cola to go with it and take everything up into the cockpit. It turns out to be a quiet meal. I take my food up to the rail with me. That way, I do not have to interrupt my lookout duties for a long time.

"It's hopeless," I whisper, "this huge, endless sea. Hopeless."

Actually, it is beyond hopeless now. We have clearly failed. Our search has failed! That's enough to drive me crazy.

"Anyhow," says Alex, "they are no longer on the beaches or at the reef. Their small boat is not to be found anywhere."

"Now, we must continue our search ashore."

Judging by the strange look which Alex gives me, he does not think that this is such a good idea.

We move a few miles further northward, past San Pedro.

"We know that they wanted to go South," Alex says, "But we know, as they are women...well, maybe they decided to do things differently at short notice."

I don't respond to such a stupid comment. But he is right, everyone can decide to do things differently at times.

So, we still make a good deal of headway in a northerly direction. But there are too many roads, houses and people along this coast. Someone would have found the girls, for sure.

Dog-tired and totally disappointed, we drive through the reef passage and into the lagoon with the last of the daylight. The anchor manoeuvre takes place already in the twilight, which is, however, no problem since we already know everything here, at our favourite place. We go through the necessary actions almost automatically.

Alex sits down at the radio and contacts the village police station for any new messages. He reports about our unsuccessful search and promises the Chief of Police, whose urgent requests sound rather like commands, to refrain from further searches, or at least to coordinate these with him first.

"My, wasn't he angry, that big headed, pompous prick!"

"Come on, Alex, don't get excited, he can't stop us looking around. But you're right, he does act weird. And that he's somehow not kosher, that's something we already know. Shady. That's almost certainly the same one I saw with the girls. And he pretends as if..."

"You couldn't have seen that exactly from a distance."

"Yes, I know, I'm much too tired for – Yes, for espionage and all that. But I want to keep looking anyway — tomorrow!"

After a cup of noodle soup of the kind "just add water" and a slice of bread, we retreat to our bunk.

I snuggle into the warm armpit of Alex, at my favourite angle, and I feel good. At home.

Nevertheless, I sigh deeply. Alex understands me.

"All will be well again, the girls have to be somewhere. And nothing major can happen to them, really. Even Belize is no longer a wild jungle or a dangerous wilderness. It is a civilized country with..."

"... with theft on the agenda, with a police force that skims off their share, with a slave trade, at least as far as babies are concerned, with child prostitution, drug crimes, corruption...!"

"...all crimes that happen here just as much as in our beautiful Europe. Yes, well, perhaps not exactly everything and also not to the same extent, but the girls know about such dangers, they are not stupid, and...Let's just hope for the best!"

"But you know what I find strangest, most of all...?"

"Hm..."

"...that we did not see a police boat or a squad looking for the girls anywhere today!"

"That is really strange, as though they knew exactly..."

For a long time, I am unable to fall asleep because I'm not just worried – I'm really scared.

Great, terrible fear is what I have inside me...and worry over what happened to the two girls.

# The shady village policeman flexes his muscle

As always, I am the first one to be awake. "Listen, Alex, there's a motorboat coming."

I punch Alex in his side, "Wake up, can't you hear?"

"Yes, of course," he moans. "How could I not hear it? It's certainly loud enough. You are too. Much too loud for someone like me, who would like to sleep in peace a bit longer."

Alex squints, sits up and looks up to the hatch. But I've already gotten up, slipped into my clothes, and now I hurry outside. Before Alex can even stretch his head out of the hatch, I have already tied up one of the large fenders, so that the police vehicle, which has by now almost arrived at our boat, can moor alongside, without scratching the side of the hull. Before Alex can say or ask anything at all, three policemen are on the *Seeschwalbe* with a murmured "g'day" and "sorry."

Mel David, the chief of the village police, is muttering something about "a missing girl" and "looking for a girl."

He is standing in the cockpit, bullish and broad legged, and barks instructions at his people. He orders them to search the boat thoroughly and his men directly set out to do so.

And how! They trample across the deck and climb into the boat. Alex and I are first standing there bewildered, then I start to protest and Alex asks loudly if that would actually be permissible, to simply come aboard just like that.

"We asked first," the chief of police claimed. "You did not say no, and so, we came on board. In addition, we are investigating an important police matter, and so, you have to allow us on board."

His men trample around everywhere and stare in each box, as if a girl could hide herself in there. They take the liberty to lift up the floorboards, to push the dresses back and forth in the lockers and even to raise the mattresses on the beds.

"Pompous guy," I grumble furiously and follow the men, in order to make sure they don't break or take anything during the search.

"I don't trust those boorish dudes at all."

I now place myself beside David and listen exactly to what he says. I get thoughtful, "But that is strange, Alex. The good man is speaking of *one* girl, or did I get that wrong with my poor English? — looking for a girl — a missing girl — that is singular?"

Alex shrugs his shoulders and I turn to the chief, "Do you know something? You know something about one of the two girls. Has one returned, and you are looking for only *one* of them now?"

The police chief spins round to face me. "What are you saying, dammit?"

He has gone completely red in the face. A red black guy, that looks bizarre and dangerous. His eyes are flashing with anger.

I say, "Yes," explaining, "You speak of looking for only *one* girl, looking for a girl...?"

Mel David raises his voice, "I tell you something, I tell you something, don't interfere. Your spying, search operations... and now you claim that I am lying. We are looking for *two* girls, I know of nothing else! Two girls, two!"

He gesticulates around in front of my nose with his two outstretched fingers, and his voice gets loud and sharp, not at all adjusted to the situation. Except, he has really just made a mistake with — *one* girl?

Alex pushes me aside and plants himself squarely in front of the police chief. The two men are about the same size, but the chief of police seems twice as massive, because of his enormous width. And three times as dangerous, because of his rage.

However, Alex can make just as much of a fuss. He lifts up his square jaw, staring the commissioner in the face with an angry look, puts his hands on his hips and makes something clear.

"Now, you listen to me," his English is perfect and his words come out quietly, but very clearly. "You have nothing to shout about around here. We know Sabine and Katharina, and we have a right to know whether something happened and if so, what. And we will not let anything or anybody discourage us to do what we think is right. If we have the feeling that we can help somehow — for example by searching, or something else — then we will do it!"

The chief of police gets quieter, turns round and murmurs something like — finished! He tells his men to get off the ship. Then, he gives a few instructions, not because his men might not know how one transfers from a sailing boat into the police boat, but only in order to show them who is boss.

Alex holds the police chief back and says quietly, so that his people cannot hear him: "Today, all day long, we will restrain ourselves. But if we do not hear anything new about the two girls by this evening, then I will personally make a request for investigation with the state police in the capital."

That hit home. This time, the chief of police grows pale. A pale black guy. Somehow, he looks much worse — and much more dangerous. Subdued, the man leaves the *"Seeschwalbe."*

"Alex, I'm afraid. This Mel David knows something, he is somehow involved there and he wants to find the girls — or should one say, 'the girl', and then, what about the other one? Everything's so puzzling. I'm really afraid."

Alex puts his arm around my shoulder, "You know what, I also have a really strange feeling. Not only you — this time. I think that we're not going to remain alone out here on the boat."

He looks at his watch, "It will be eight o'clock soon, and we will now treat ourselves to the luxurious breakfast buffet and a cosy day of reading, swimming and lazing about at the hotel resort. There, we will be mingling with the nice people and will immediately hear about it, if something comes to light about the girls. And if, by evening, nothing new has happened, I swear to you that I will personally call the police in the capital. Is that also in your interest?" He looks at me affectionately with his faithful, brown eyes.

Then a serious expression comes into his warm brown eyes, "But, Sandra love, there's something you have to promise me. We are not going to spy, not even the tiniest, smallest, next to nothing amount, not the whole, long, beautiful day! "

"But we could…?"

"No buts!"

"You know we can speak to the hotel manager again, that is my *but*. He knows more about Kati and Biene than he is letting on, I'm quite sure …"

"Agreed, we shall speak to the hotel manager…*both of us*. But, otherwise, we do not do anything except laze about, promise?"

"No, no, nothing else," I promise and start to run, in order to fetch my bathing suit and my book.

I don't need to tell good Alex now that I will also chat a little with the other guests, for sure. I will talk to the handsome barman Duky and, naturally, I am also going to find out what the nice tour guide Sandy knows.

But why worry dear Alex?

# Village trip with consequences

That is not for me...simply hanging around at the resort in such a way.

Naturally, swimming is relaxing, reading is distracting and the lavish breakfast is, of course, a stunner. My stomach extends even more now and feels like a watermelon. Each time, I decide not to gorge out at the buffet, but with this wide selection of delicacies, it is always more than I intended to eat, without exception.

Also, the discussions with Sandy, Hal Morgan and Duky were extremely interesting and showed me different perspectives again, of how the people here want to deal with their lives and the future.

Hal tells us about his future resort in the most colourful images. His broad smile is back on his face and his eyes sparkle.

He wants to redecorate and enlarge everything. To the existing pool, a larger more luxurious one should be added, the garden is to become a jungle-like park and a concert hall will round off the whole plan. Also, a long dock with a beach bar and an even more modern dive centre will be built — that is the plan. His face lights up with excitement, and I assume he is mentally already in the midst of his glory.

Frowningly, I look about myself. How will Hal pay for it all? The resort is now barely half full, during the main season! Well, maybe he's just one of these rich Americans who settle anywhere in the Caribbean.

Just as I want to ask a question about the costs, Alex pre-empts me, "This will cost enormous sums...your resort...it is doing that well?"

"Ha...very good..." he laughs.

Even Duky, whom we are talking to now, has his dreams. Even these, as he tells us, go in an expensive direction. He wants to open his own bar in Belize City, and become world-famous with his own creations — colourful, imaginative drinks. With Duky, I can imagine that the government could contribute something from their promotion fund. But enough for his own bar in the capital?

We still talk to various guests and employees.

We learn a lot of interesting things, but nothing new about the girls, except that they really have disappeared; that no one had seen them after they had set out for their trip.

All these are naturally no real pieces of news, of course, but confirm my suspicion that something terrible must have happened to them. This is not a case of just getting lost or a voluntary disappearance.

Where did the two children go? Where could they have run to, after they disappeared into the mangroves? Ambergris Cay is not all that huge.

Did they hide out in the mangroves, to wait until the men had gone, in order to then disappear with their wooden boat? Did helpful people hide them? In the meantime, however, they would have had to resurface, no matter from where.

Or – or are Kati and Biene still afraid of these men? And don't dare to venture out from their hiding place?

This soul-searching is making me sick. I cannot just sit around here, uselessly. I think I'd much rather take a stroll through the village of San Pedro. Perhaps one could hear something there...

"Alex...," I ask, "are you coming along?"

His resistant glance and the demonstrative hiding behind the "Belize news" immediately gives me my answer.

"Very well," I say, "then I'm just going to stroll alone into the village." Next, I gather my stuff together and I get up.

"Sandra, Sassi!"

Whenever he is angry with me, he calls me by my full name. His warning is probably intended to hold me back, but in my current mood, nothing and no-one is going to stop me.

"A harmless stroll, I shall not spy or investigate. And I did not send the fax to Lisa either yet."

My feet start to run. My eyes target the goal. But stop, where did the path to the village go? I pause, thinking first.

I turn and see Alex standing there, beside the small table. He is grinning all over his entire, cheeky face. He does not have to say anything. I already know it myself. Once again, my brain had only switched on after starting to run off.

Lie – start – run

Alex pulls me towards the dinghy and mumbles, "Come with me, it's easier than going by the dusty road."

In peaceful union, we stroll through the village of San Pedro. Alex now also enjoys the walk. What we see, we like very much. The simple timber buildings are surrounded by pretty gardens, which are fenced with flowering hedges and planted with palm trees. The facilities are lovingly maintained, which certainly cannot be said of the houses. The wobbly walls and inclined roofs often seem to be held together only by the paint, which has been wastefully distributed and comes in remarkable and shrill colour tones. Particularly, the colours of pink, mint and sky-blue shine through everywhere between the shrubs. As a result, the whole village has a very cheerful and really exotic appearance. Looking through one of the always open doors into the rooms, one sees very simple furniture and everywhere — under the tables, on the beds or on the staircase — there are children. The future of these families and therefore of the village is secured.

Children are everywhere; laughing, screaming children.

The village paths that meander between the colourful wooden houses, consist of white sand, trampled down firmly. Even "the main street" is a sandy road, but onto which they have slapped a few loads of gravel, that with time, have been compressed into a hard surface by the cars.

I can only see smaller children, the large ones are bound to be at school. Women are hanging up laundry on lines that are stretched between the houses and palm trees. Several men are sitting together on the stairs or on the enclosed, dusty village square.

"I wonder whether those people have nothing better to do all day long than to gossip — apologies — for men, this is called a debate."

Alex, who wants to defend himself and his gender, says condescendingly, "Those guys were surely out fishing all night, while the women squatted, watched television or were gossiping."

We like these people. Belize boasts a wide range of skin colours and types.

First of all, there are the descendants of the Aboriginals, the Mayas, but these tend to be living in the hinterland of Belize. Then, there are the mestizos, descendants of Spanish conquerors mixed with Mayas. A group of Garifunas are living in the South on the coast. They are former Black slaves, who had mixed with the indigenous Caribs and had been deported here from the Caribbean Islands. However, the majority of the population is made up of black descendants of the slaves, and of the Creoles, also former black slaves, who had mixed with

Europeans. In San Pedro, the residents are almost exclusively members of the latter group. So, you can see brown and black in all shades.

"You know what surprises me a bit?" I ask Alex and give him the answer, "The people here do not seem to have much. The desolate huts and rather meagre dresses...but, suddenly, you see modern radio and TV and — look there — a big car."

"Now that you say that. But perhaps one or the other has a good job?"

"A job that is good enough to buy all these things?"

"There are people with money in every society...wherever it came from."

"Exactly...the "from where" is what I am wondering about."

Alex looks at me searchingly, but says nothing more.

Belize is the only country in Central America where English is officially spoken. Belize had been a British colony for a long time, and only became independent in 1981. Since that time, however, it has still been part of the Commonwealth. And, one can also assume, gladly so, as all the pictures of the Queen in every store, in all official offices, and even in some private living rooms. But perhaps this is only the outward appearance, which can be deceptive. In the minds of the people...I think, you can't see what is going on there.

You can't even see into the head of my good Alex, because while I have revolutionary, earth-shattering thoughts, such as colonialism, slavery and other things, my good Alex, once again, only has very profane things on his mind. He wipes his forehead and groans, "Oh no, I'm hellishly thirsty again. I hope there's a place to get something to drink in this village that resembles a baking oven."

"I guess, my poor Alex, that you really will not die of thirst. But first, let's get all these things done that we've set out to do."

The main point, which is the tour of San Pedro, is done quickly. I decide to send the fax to Lisa from the post office, which takes a good quarter of an hour. In the two small souvenir shops, I decide to roam around a little and buy my indispensable sweets. Alex gets a small can with gasoline for the dinghy at the gas station. Soon, we are done and stroll down to the beach.

We walk past a two-storey house, one of the few solidly built houses in the village. It looks as though it has to exert extraordinary force just to hold the two floors. One above the other, it stands there, skewed and ratty, underneath a huge mango tree. But it is, nevertheless, a real house and not just a painted cottage.

Posters on the exterior walls advertise alcohol, coke and colourful fruit juices. Of course, Alex's thirst now immediately increases to skyrocket proportions. Purposefully, he's heading to the entrance — pulling me behind him with his hand.

Underneath the doorway, he turns around and peaks through the hanging branches of the big mango tree towards the beach that is just...over there. The house is not far from the shore and we can even see the *Seeschwalbe* from here. It lies peacefully in the calm water in the bay out there in the deep blue sea, just about as far from the resort as from the village. The bar is actually the one that we have seen — and heard — from the boat. The multicoloured lights are off now, but I can see the light chains hanging up in the mango tree.

Soon, we are sitting at one of the simple wooden tables, with our cans of beer or cola in front of us, and conversing with the indescribably fat, chatty, coal-black and cheerful woman behind the counter. Ana is an extremely bubbly and talkative woman.

In the bar, the obligatory picture of the young, pretty and pink-dressed Queen Elizabeth of England is hanging up on the wall.

Ana chats on, lively and nearly without interruption, and wants to know everything about us. From where, when, why, how and where to? Laughing, we responded to Ana's questions during one of the breaks in her rambling. We listen to the complete story of good Ana's life, although we doubt the number and the extent of the described adventures somewhat. But it's still interesting and above all, entertaining. We say good-bye, with the bartender lady's promise not to put the music on full blast anymore in the evening and with the firm promise on our side to drop by again soon.

We had not thought, however, that it would be so soon. As we reach our dinghy, we notice, in fact, that everything in it is missing.

"All cleaned out!" yells Alex, "fucking gang!"

The dinghy is lying in the scorching sun, totally stripped bare. Engine, tank, cover, bench, rudder — they took everything. Alex immediately trudges back across the beach again, dragging me after him by the hand, and here we are, before we know it, back in the bar. Poor Ana has to listen to Alex's anger and frustration. The bartender recommends that we report it all to the chief of the local police, Mr. David, "Although," she adds anxiously and rolls her eyes meaningfully, "that will not be much use, either."

Still, we do this immediately. The police chief of the San Pedro branch, Mel David, nods seriously, notes the complaint, promises with lots of gesticulating to do everything humanly possible, and files the report away in his bottom drawer. Most likely, I fear, the drawer for unpleasant cases. Never to be seen again...

Back on the beach, near the bar, we see fat Ana standing at the door and beckoning us to come in again.

She hands us some old, heavy oars, so that we can at least return to our sailboat. She also promises she will ask around a bit, "...which will be better than waiting for the police." Pompously, she pats herself on her heaving chest, and then on her ears, "I promise, I have good ears, better than the police."

Asking around ends with Ana and two young men, her nephews, she says, arriving at our boat in an old rowing boat, late in the evening, and bringing along everything, engine, tank, oars and bench.

Ana laughs all over her face, slapping herself on the thigh with delight, and occasionally calling out: "...and half of the stuff is stacked away in the crested bend behind the police station!"

"Are there any things they had already found there and had secured?" I ask harmlessly.

Ana blurts out, "That's funny — secured — sorry, but that is really precious!"

The two guys are also laughing gleefully and one of them exclaims, "...secured, one can probably say, it is certainly as secure there as anywhere else! It's with the police, but still not safe enough for Ana."

Alex and I are looking at each other. Well, we don't particularly find this funny. Why with the police? Why safe, but not for Ana? But now that we have all our things back again, we won't ask any more questions. The boys stow the stuff away in the tender of the *Seeschwalbe* and accept the invitation to come on board for a drink. Surprisingly nimble for her weight, Ana climbs over the rail and plants herself down on the cushions in the cockpit. We spend a very enjoyable evening with each other, with a few chilled bottles of beer, and celebrate the wonder of the discovery of the stolen goods.

The thing with the police keeps going through my head.

"Is…," I start off, "... the police not so very…I mean – Oh, what's the name in English – I mean fair? Clean?"

Ana understands what I mean and regretfully shakes her head. Then she puts one of her fat fingers to her pursed lips. That is answer enough for us.

Here with Ana and two boys, who have plonked themselves down casually in the corners of the cockpit, we learn much more about the real thoughts of the Belizers now, about such things as authority, corruption, colonialism, independence and racial problems.

Ana seems to be content with her life. She has an income from her bar and is respected in the village. She explains this to us with a laugh.

Stan and Roby, the nephews of Ana, tell us some more unpleasant things. She tells us of Chinese shop owners who refuse to give them a job, because they are Christian; of officials who refuse them documents before they have tipped them. And this or that, in which they are being disadvantaged, because they are not the right colour, religion or status. In Belize City, they have nothing to say, anyway, because they come from the village.

So many obstacles; such tremendous discrimination in one's own country.

But the missing will, perhaps, also plays a small role? Is it perhaps the case that the proverbial Caribbean flair stands in the way of a career for the young men?

Why do the enterprises and hotels in San Pedro need to recruit their employees from outside the country? I almost only ever see workers from China, the US, or neighbouring countries, such as Guatemala and Honduras. At the resort, I know only Duky, who originates from Belize, and naturally, some of the women. The waitresses, the chambermaids and the kitchen helpers are mostly local women.

I assume that the Caribbean idleness is confined to men. Particularly to young men, because the elderly or old ones go fishing, or make souvenirs out of coral, which they then sell.

Am I being too hard on them? Too mean? Surely everyone can live as he pleases. But then, why complain or seek the blame elsewhere? That doesn't add up.

"And how do you see the future of your country, Ana? Now that you have your independence from Great Britain, and have had it already for a few years?"

"No problem," she laughs, carefree, "things will go on somehow, the Lord in heaven...well, and our exports are booming, and tourism also. So many new things are being planned. Hotels, a new bridge...in a few years, no-one will recognize San Pedro anymore."

Ana's eyes flash with sheer joy for the future, "...all the money that flows into Belize through tourists or the export trade comes to us — to the little people. We are already getting small start-up aid for this and that...well, if the money...via the authorities...surely soon..."

Her voice trails off in a hesitant babble.

"And what about you two?" I turn to Stan and Roby. "Isn't there a ton of work on these new projects? At the construction sites, or in the new hotels?"

Both shrug in unison, "We haven't learned anything about that yet."

Not learn, I want to call out, you can learn anything. But I remain silent, what can you say?

Then the subject is changed and Ana's mood is changing back to top form. Little anecdotes are told and they all laugh, plentifully and loudly. They are laughing when we do not understand the Belize dialect, and we are laughing even louder when our guests do not understand the Swiss-tinted English, but the laughter is loudest when we truly understand each other's jokes. And there is singing, especially later in the evening, as soon as the alcohol content in the blood of our guests has reached a certain level. Alex has retrieved wine and beer from the depths of the storage boxes and has even found another half bottle of rum. Soon, he will be at the end of his supplies.

Ana laughs the loudest and the most of all of them. Her dark voice is certain to be heard across all San Pedro. And she finally also explains to us now, the background of the theft and the problems of the police. Mel, the village police chief, and his men, were still the biggest thieves. And the stolen loot was already there, but just safe from Alex and Sandra. Only Ana can take the liberty to do such a thing and just pick out the stuff from the police. She knows things…so she can take the liberty, can actually take quite a few liberties. Proudly, she tells us that, but what she knows that is so mysterious — that is something she does not tell. She only rolls her eyes heavenward and eloquently nods her head.

It's unfortunate, I think. It would certainly have been interesting.

So, we continue singing and drinking until even the last bottle cannot surrender even one more drop.

Of course, the disappearance of the girls is also being extensively discussed, but Ana turns quiet and sad. "Those poor girls. But why couldn't these stupid children remain at the resort, where it's nice and they were safe?"

The nephews are both of the opinion that a kidnapping has taken place — that would make lots of money — and the girls would suddenly emerge again. If the rich Americans…

"They are Germans."

To many natives, all rich white tourists are simply Americans.

"…Once the rich parents have paid up."

And now — it is around two o'clock in the morning and Ana has to swing her weight back over the rail, which happens with less energy and elegance than it did at her arrival. With vigorous waving, the three revellers disappear into the darkness of the warm tropical night.

Alex clears away the empty bottles of a whole week's ration. "Hm," he wonders, "just as well that the woman owns a bar. She could otherwise hardly cover even her own needs."

"Maybe she doesn't usually drink as much, not when it comes out of her own supplies?"

# No fun dive

The next day is another day of waiting around for any news of Katharina and Sabine. Since I myself am not allowed to become active, there remains only one thing for me to do: twiddling my thumbs and just waiting it out.

I would have a few ideas about what I could do, of course, but Alex watches me much too well.

"Sandra," my dear Alex says ponderously, "the safety of the crew is the concern of the skipper."

"Also outside the boat? When shopping and all that?"

"Oh, that's boring. My nerves are not suited at all for reading or hanging out on the boat. I have to keep busy."

"When, Alex, when do you actually want to call the state police?"

"I already did so yesterday, from the gas station."

"Why didn't you tell me?"

"Now I've told you."

By themselves, my naughty eyes roll skyward, "And? Do tell, finally."

"Not much to tell. I just had them connect me to a drug investigation specialist. And he, this Jonson, he said he was the boss. I told him that two tourists had disappeared in San Pedro. And that we think, well, that the village police are not taking this matter very seriously."

"Hm. Yes, that should do it. You did that anonymously."

"Sure. I didn't want to endanger us. One never knows."

The sun is already high up in the dark-blue sky, and so I decide at short notice to take a guided tour of the coral reef on one of the boats from the resort.

Alex has no desire to go diving. After I promised him, cross my heart and hope to die, not to spy or otherwise put myself in danger, he lets me go.

Quickly, I gather up my stuff and then race to the resort by dinghy, where I can just about arrange with the diving instructor to fill a set of bottles for me.

"Do you have a diving licence?"

"Of course. Here you go – PADI, with all the bells and whistles."

I don't tell him that I haven't been diving for a long time. Possibly, he would have taken me ashore for a practice session for an hour and would not have taken me now. In the first of the three diving boats, there was still room for me.

We pass through the middle of the lagoon. The water is very clear and sparkles in all shades of turquoise and blue. We reach the passage in the reef, drive a few miles south at the edge of the reef, because we're going on to the slightly sloping reef drop in the southern region of Ambergris. The skat card player group from the resort, the Alert couple, and also Franz and Lea, the fiftieth anniversary honeymooners from Bonn, have especially requested it. At this reef drop, there are ideal places to dive at different depths...that was what they had explained to me. That is also quite alright by me.

The diving groups on the two other boats have dedicated themselves to the northern part, and that way, we will remain by ourselves. We reach our diving site and fasten an extra buoy intended especially for this purpose.

The people begin to put on their fins, put their diving masks around their necks, and then, with a skilful hip swing, they put on their lead belts and slide them into the vests already weighed down with the heavy bottles — they mutually help each other while doing this. I do exactly the same — but I have to watch the others a bit, because it really has been far too long since I was last on a dive. Mark, the diving instructor, who has noticed my initial uncertainty, now helps me with the preparations and quickly checks my knowledge of the safety rules.

Only now that everyone is done with their preparations, does Mark give us a sign — we pull our masks over our faces and then, always in pairs, start to plop backwards into the water, respectively one on each side of the boat. Then, one after the other, the divers give Mark o.k. signs and swim along behind him. Soon, the point has been reached where Mark wants to do some exercises with us.

"No pain, no gain," he says.

After tarring, bobbing up and down, and breathing exercises, we get impatient, however. Everyone wants to go on, and finally experience something.

Almost every diver has a waterproof camera hanging around their neck. Some of the devices also feature a sophisticated underwater flash system and accurate search devices.

Soon we are on our way, moving slowly as we inform each other of the location of lobsters, mussels, crabs, or beautiful corals and enjoy this wonderful, diverse underwater world. What we get to see makes us marvel. To describe this is impossible...we are lacking the words, which, anyway, are not at our disposal as a means of expression underwater. So we make good use of our hands, in order to show our diving buddies the glories we have just discovered.

Slowly and ever advancing, we let ourselves slide down at the steep drop, as we see new, interesting things again and again.

This incredible diversity. An orgy of colours and original shapes, never seen before.

Huge, orange, fan-shaped funnels alternate with tube-shaped, coral tubes, well over two metres high. Slightly wavy, purple brain corals are seen next to a burgundy antler coral. There are shellfish, and crabs and lobsters that flee into deep crevices, and circling around everything are countless, different types of fish.

How boring our world above the water surface truly is, when compared against the splendour down here!

We have reached the outermost point of the reef now and it is time to return. Mark gives us the appropriate sign, and he gestures at the same time that we will take a route back that leads us into a lower depth, so as not to dive the same stretch of water twice. Amazing, what he can tell us, and all of us to each other, merely by using hand signals. So, we ascend slowly and then swim towards the boat with calm fin strokes, in approximately ten metres of depth.

And there, still about a good two hundred metres away from our dive boat, we make a horrific discovery.

Floating between the corals, we discover the girl, Katharina.

She looks like a mermaid. Her white, slender body is surrounded by orange coral fronds swaying gently to and fro, her fine, silvery hair waves gently along with the current and her blue eyes stare towards the sun-drenched surface, as though searching. The fluorescent, turquoise-green water throws small, rippling waves across her skin, which shimmers white and greenish and gleams like her white shirt. The delicate blue Pareo supports the magical impression. A watercolour painting in gentle shades; a work of art, full of peace and beauty.

The ugly scar that gapes in red at the temple of the girl, disturbs the peaceful image and we realize that the quiet peace is eternal.

Panic erupts immediately.

Fortunately, we are no longer at a great depth, otherwise some of the diving buddies would have had major problems. Because many of them now forget all the rules of correct ascending and shoot up, much too fast, to the water surface, where they are left struggling, gasping for air, and fidgeting about.

In my first fright, I clasp at the corals and stare at Katharina, rigid with fear and as though stunned.

Another holiday resort guest, Franz Stalder, has also remained behind, down below. Stalder keeps himself steady at Katharina's level and photographs her from all sides.

Mark, who accompanied the dive group up and back to the boat, has returned and makes the sign for us to ascend. On the surface of the water, he marks the discovery site of the corpse with a small emergency buoy, which he anchors on a long leash on the coral next to the dead girl. Then he swims to the boat with us.

Franz sits down beside Mark, "...at home in Frankfurt, I work as a forensic doctor," he says softly, "and I thought that photos might be necessary. I'm just telling you, so that you're not wondering why I was able to be so calm in doing this. For me, something like that is, unfortunately, nearly an everyday sight."

Mark, reassured, now looks at me, quizzically. I do not have such a good answer ready and therefore, I say nothing. I must admit the fact that I was just in shock and was therefore unable to pry my clasping fingers loose from the corals.

On the way home, no-one says a word.

Quiet and subdued, all of us retreat to our rooms and the employees are instructed to bring coffee, tea, tranquillisers or whatever people ask them to.

A police boat with divers immediately goes out to the site, in order to recover the body of the poor girl and take it to forensics.

Depressed, I return to our sailboat, sit down in my favourite corner in the living room, which today, however, offers neither comfort nor protection to me. Crying, I report the circumstances of Kati's death to Alex.

Katharina, the sweet, pretty Kati, she had looked like a mermaid in a fairy tale, white and silent and beautiful.

And then the ugly scar, "...then, it's suddenly not a fairy tale. Not any more."

Alex sits down beside me and hugs me.

...Kati...I think...Kati...she...Kati...mermaid...corals... scar...Kati.... is dead. D E A D!!!

And then, suddenly, it occurs to me, "Alex, and what about Sabine? What if they also find Sabine like that? Where is the poor child?"

Somehow, I have the gut feeling that Biene is still alive. Perhaps it is, however, only the urgent desire that I want it to be like that, which gives me this gut feeling. And yet...maybe?

And now, I still...somewhat...suddenly, it becomes clear to me, clear as daylight breaking through the night, "...Katharina, she died...but not today...and the police Chief, Mel David, he knew, and therefore on our boat...of *one* girl...did he only speak of one...yes, he did."

"missing a girl" and "looking for a girl"

Alex, understanding, looks me in the eye and holds me tight.

# A song for children and old ladies

"I'm gonna go shopping...into the village!"

I'm already dressed and ready to go. I have already swung one of my jean-clad legs over the railing and before Alex can react, I'm sitting in the dinghy. I want to go alone. I have a suspicion, or — as Alex would say — a gut feeling, and I want to investigate it.

I suspect Sabine is in the village. Now that we've found Kati, it's even more important that Biene is found, too. She probably saw the killers of Kati, she knows what happened.

I want to go to three different places and the first of these is the police station. It is clear to me that paying a visit to the village police station is dangerous. But just like that, in broad daylight, the chief of police is not going to have me killed.

The second place I want to investigate is the store. In the basement, that is something I've seen, they have got a large storage room. There, I must look...absolutely.

Finally, I want to go to the bar. The bar above all, because already twice, at night when I couldn't sleep, I had seen something peculiar there that perked my curiosity.

The first time had been in early evening, two days ago, because I had seen two shapes at the top window. A fat one — no question, whose figure that was — and a slender one, which had disappeared again immediately.

And last night, when I had been sitting outside, at approximately eleven o'clock, and the house had been dark...only down in the bar area, there was a solitary light.

The outside lights had been switched off and that had never happened before, ever since we had been here, at the bay. Every evening, otherwise, this flashing jumble/tangle of multicoloured lights had been on, even on Sunday.

Red – blue – yellow.

Ana doesn't have a rest day. And when the lights go out in the evening, then the shutters are closed immediately. But yesterday, that didn't happen. There were no lights on in the house, except for the small, weak lamp. No multicoloured fixed lighting outside. And half of the shutters were open.

I must find out, naturally, what is going on. I must look around and I have to do this alone. I have no use for Alex in this.

I get hold of the dinghy before Alex can react at all. He hastens up the walkway and now he is already hanging his body over the railing, "Wait, I'm gonna come along!"

However, I prevent this by pushing off in the dinghy, getting the engine going and then I am already far enough that he cannot catch up with me. Swim ashore he might, but I'm sure that this is something he won't do.

I don't look back, of course. I don't want to see his angry face. It will be enough to deal with him once I get back.

Just when I am walking in between the trees towards the police station, I can see Duky standing in the doorway and whispering with the chief of police.

What's the handsome Duky doing here? A firm handshake is being exchanged, serious nodding, then Duky disappears around the corner. Inside, in the station, I meet the chief, Mel David.

Pretending to be clueless, I ask him many questions about the things that were stolen from our dinghy. I ask him whether he already knew anything about the thief. Why only, for God's sake, had the thief deposited his loot in the police crest, and whether such thefts occurred often, and then I asked a thousand other things. Mr. David pumps himself up, belly in, chest out. The arrogant man casts condescending looks down at me from his eyes that are towering above me. In his quirky English, he makes numerous excuses, provides explanations, and then more reports of success in his work. With his twitching, thick eyebrows, he underlines the importance of his words. It would be an impressive show...if I didn't know just how seriously he really takes his work.

Unfortunately, I do not understand everything all the time, due to his Belize-tainted English, but I understand the basic idea perfectly. He speaks fast and says — nothing. I get a lot more information about this man through the appearance of his wife Rosalita...I do not even need good English skills. Through the large window on the rear wall, I can see her climbing down from the first floor, using a wide spiral staircase, then she walks through the park-like gardens and enters the office through the back door. Or better said, floats.

"Do you have your private apartment upstairs?" I ask the police chief.

"Hm, yes... it is practical."

Then he will certainly not be hiding Biene. In his apartment, and with this wife! A smashing woman! And expensive. The value of her jewellery alone...I could have lived on that for a full year. Then the complex plaited hair-style, with a golden, tastefully crafted bangles. The fine fabric of her dress and the perfect makeup. She extracts her wallet from her beautiful leather handbag and checks whether she has enough money. The police chief pulls out his own wallet immediately and fishes out a couple of bills. The beautiful wife thanks him, sweetly, "Adios mi Amor, see you this evening."

Is this beauty a mestizia from Belize? Rather, I think she is a Latina from Guatemala or Honduras. There are such beautiful women among them and they are highly desired among men the world over, including in Belize. The luxurious woman nods at me slightly and — leaving a perfume cloud behind her — floats out of the mundane office of her husband.

Astonished, my glance follows her. The wife of a village policeman?

However, that was at least a clear answer to one of my most important questions about this shady chief of police. Has he maybe got a small, lucrative sideline business? He must have. With this woman!

"Do you have prison cells at the police station?" This question flashes through my head, and I ask it immediately.

"Not enough room, no basement. They go directly to Belmopan... the crooks."

With a nod, I say goodbye to the chief of police, and go on into the village. At the shop, I first roam around a little, then ask for an item that I'm supposedly looking for in vain and which the nice shop assistant promises to get for me from the basement. I hurry immediately behind, of course. But except for buckets, bags and boxes, I discover nothing in the storeroom. Not even the desired item.

There are also no doors or adjoining rooms, and so, I leave the basement again, satisfied that there is nothing in there.

Upstairs, in a sales basket, I discover things like lipsticks, sunglasses and all kinds of stuff, and so, a spontaneous idea comes to me. Maybe I will have to...hmm...follow someone one day, without wanting to be recognized immediately. So I purchase a sun hat with a broad rim, and dark sun glasses with large lenses. I then ask to have all this wrapped in a plastic bag. Alex does not need to see the strange items that I am going to come home with.

As I shoot around the corner of the store, I can see, who would believe it, the tour guide, Sandy, who disappears again behind the nearest bushes...with a bowl in her hand. Already twice before, I had noticed that she snuck away with dishes from the resort. Naturally, I'm running behind her and I'm just in time to see Sandy slip into a small, simple house. Undecided, I'm looking around, and then I continue to stroll on, as though I had nothing better to do than stroll along. And really, behind the timber building, Sandy is sitting on a step of the porch and watches a small girl of approximately five years of age, as she, with a brownish-smeared mouth, eats out of the bowl that Sandy had brought along. Chocolate pudding. The smeared chocolate is only a trace darker than the skin of the child. Is that Sandy's secret? This child?

A five-year-old girl — and not a trace of Sabine! There, I had imagined something again. But actually, I scold myself, that was a stupid idea of mine in the first place, to think that Sandy would have hidden Sabine somewhere. Despite all the secrecy, that would be much too public a location. Here, in the midst of the village, just a few minutes away from the police station. And why, for God's sake, would Sandy do such a thing?

I should have better thoroughly considered the matter, rather than simply be chasing behind Sandy.

Once again, my legs had been faster than the brain.

I want to retreat, unnoticed, but Sandy discovers me and jumps up, frightened. She positions herself protectively in front of the little girl, as though I would not have already since long have seen the child.

"Sandy," I say, softly, "I'm sorry, I didn't want to follow you...I mean, yes...I wanted to, but...I thought, I mean..."

Oh, how ashamed I am of my snooping around. Alex is often right, despite everything! Because, this time, I have been very wrong.

"Please, don't say a word at the hotel, they will fire me immediately," Sandy implores me, fearfully.

"But, what am I not allowed to say because, I...?"

Sandy steps aside and answers quietly: "Cleo is my daughter. I took her along from Martinique. I had no right to do that. She is now living here with an old couple and I sometimes bring her something special to eat from the hotel kitchen," Sandy looks at me, pleadingly.

"Sandy, you don't have to worry, I certainly won't tell."

Musingly, I look at little Cleo, and now I can see that the child bears a striking resemblance to Sandy. The same light chocolate skin, the black, slightly slanted eyes, the dark hair.

"Hello Cleo, how are you?" I have to dig out my French from the remotest corners of my brain because the little girl from Martinique only speaks that.

"Ça va, merci," the child replies politely, "would you like some chocolate pudding?"

I have to smile, "No, thanks, you go ahead and eat..." and then I turn to Sandy and I ask her: "Does the child like it here? And you? Do you always have to sneak about in such a way?"

"Yes, unfortunately, and no, Madame, the child does not like it here."

She told me that she would much prefer to go back home again but there is not enough money yet. Back home, she had family who longed for the child, and at some point, she would succeed in returning there. She was just, well, she had come here for a man, and now it was over...but as soon as she could, she would go home again. "Nearly all of the money for the flight is already available, and perhaps there will be enough by the end of the season. If I can stay at the hotel, where I am earning good money, and if Madame, please, would be good enough to say nothing about this at the hotel."

Of course I promise her that. I say good-bye to Sandy and the child, whereby I come away with a brown, five-finger chocolate thumbprint on my white blouse as a reminder of that encounter.

You and your spy nose that sticks itself into anything, you are a really great team, I scold myself. You so have been barking up the wrong tree.

At the bar, I get yet another surprise.

"Ana is not here," the fat black guy in his grubby shirt mumbles. "I am the supervisor for today. Ana is saying goodbye to her friend, but afterwards, she's going to be gone... she has important matters to tend to."

He takes a deep breath, "And there will be no drinks sold here today!"

"Was she already gone last night? Everything was dark?"

"Not yet...no...she went shopping, which is why the bar had been closed."

Surprised, I look over to the house, to the window where I had believed that I had seen a slender figure, then back at the ragged man. That could not have been him.

Does Ana leave this supervisor behind here and then she just goes away? And Sabine is hidden above. That cannot be, can it? Was I mistaken also here, once more, and in such a way? I was so sure that Sabine…

However, it occurs to me that Ana is not stupid. Is Ana even much, much smarter than I think her capable of? Does she leave, in order to show everyone that she has nothing to hide in her house? It is almost unbelievable, but not impossible. And this ragged guy? Is he privy? Certainly not. He seems to be drunk all day. Is the fat Marc, perhaps, also only a cover-up?

How well this has been thought through by Ana! Smart. Unique. Now, I am really convinced that Sabine is being hidden here. But why doesn't Ana tell the police? The state police? She's afraid that the village police would find out? And she cannot go anywhere with Sabine. The road to safety is much too long, and there is danger lurking everywhere.

A brainstorm for one – I amaze myself – Sabine could – swim out to us, at night. Only, she would naturally need to know that we were that close. If she is hidden away in the house somewhere, where even the fat Marc can't discover her ...she can't look outside. Can't find an escape route for herself.

And why doesn't Ana send her out to us, then, to the boat?

The answer comes to meet me head on, in the shape of two men, who are creeping around the house corner, looking into the window and behaving so conspicuously inconspicuous that I almost have to laugh. They are snooping around in the village. They are looking for Biene!

Marc allows them into the house and lets them question him. A few minutes later, the guys seem to be satisfied and take off.

Now I am totally at a loss. Is Biene there? Or not?

But I have to warn her. If she is hidden in the house, then it's of use to her...if not, there is no harm done, either.

"May I rest a little, in the shaded house, just for a moment?"

Marc looks at me dubiously.

"...I am not feeling all that well," I add and put on a suffering face. Reluctantly, Marc bids me inside the house and allows me to sit on a stool. Then he stares at me and probably thinks, she has now totally gone crazy, because I, an otherwise reputable-looking lady, suddenly start to sing out loud in a foreign language:

"*I have a small boat,*
*that is moored not far from the beach,*

*and if one wants to visit it*
*that helps a great deal."*
A song for children or senile old ladies.
Simple, the song, but if it helps??

**Then I get up, smooth my jeans, and thank a bewildered Marc. Then I put a few coins into his hand and say, on my way out: "So! Now I am feeling so much better!"**

# Family as alibi

I have barely left the bar and Marc, when I see Ana rushing out from between the huts. I slip behind some bushes, wondering whether I should check where Ana is going to. What's so important that she has to take care of it?

Determined, she enters her bar, gets out a large bag stuffed full to the top, gives a few more instructions to Marc, waving her fingers to and fro, and then leaves her house, heading towards the village. Reluctantly, I follow her.

Because with my white blouse and my grey bob of hair, Ana might spot me already from afar, I have to do something about this. I twist my plaited hair tightly together while walking, put on the newly purchased hat and place the sun glasses on my nose. Then, I slip out of my blouse and stuff it in the plastic bag. My black top, to go with the jeans that I now quickly roll up at the leg, is almost something like a uniform here, it does not stand out.

Ana has not noticed me at all. She boards the bus, lost in thought, and sits down into the farthest corner, where she, still absent minded, is now staring out the window. So I can buy my ticket, get off at the last stop and change over to the speedboat, get on the cross-country bus to Belmopan in Belize City, behind Ana, and, once there, get off as well and follow her to a house.

Quietly, I position myself behind a hibiscus bush — blessed be these thick bushes that grow rampant everywhere in Belize – and watch Ana.

A crowd of children and a fat, black lady, who, by her appearance, must be her sister, all welcome Ana warmly.

Is this another disappointment again? Is Ana merely visiting her family? Slowly but surely, I am really getting too old for spying.

I crouch down between the hibiscus bushes and peep through the branches.

Ana embraces her sister warmly, squeezes her tight and kisses her gently on the round cheeks.

Thick lips hit on fat cheeks.

Massive wrestler's arms hug monster shoulders.

Grease rings encounter blubber tires.

The two sisters resemble sumo fighter twins.

"You're looking good ...very nice!"

"You, too!" The greeting is so loud that I can understand each and every word.

The sister steps aside and you can see a whole bunch of fidgety, darker arms and legs next to her. The balls untangle themselves and hang themselves onto Ana in the form of individual children. The children hug her and are reaching for her large bag now. Ana laughs and distributes the goodies, which she had brought with her. Then she conjures up a bottle of rum from her fathomless bag and the two sisters retire inside the house.

A visit to the sister!

But, maybe, Ana can take care of yet another important matter here?

Should the sister, whom one does not know in San Pedro yet, perhaps, report to the state police, tell them where Sabine is? Does Ana want to make a phone call from here? Doesn't she trust the telephones in the village?

With all these questions, I realize that I no longer doubt that Sabine is with Ana.

I crouch between these shrubs and feel somewhat ridiculous. But at least I have enough time in order to rethink the whole thing in peace. Thus, I list all the points:

Sabine could have only escaped from the small bay to somewhere in San Pedro.

But not into the village itself, she would have been seen in the village.

Just the same, the road through the village and into the resort would have been blocked for her.

The only three houses with proper "hiding places", like cellars or attics, are the police building, the shop and Ana's house.

Two of them would not apply.

In addition, Katharina and Sabine had met Ana.

Sabine would possibly have remembered to flee to us, onto the boat. But...at that time, we were not in the proximity of our boat, we were at Cay Caulker.

The girls must also have seen that a policeman was part of the pursuit

So, the police would be out of question for her.

Sabine saw what had happened to Kati...*no, Sandra, that is only an assumption.*

But she lost Kati.

If she's with Ana, she knows about Kati now and she also knows that she has nowhere to go.

And that she is in great danger, because she saw the policeman.

So, she will be staying in hiding at Ana's place until... just, Ana now maybe has informed the State police.

Or her sister does it.

Did I forget something, or twist it, or think along the wrong lines? My head buzzes.

In addition, it is hot, despite the shade of the blooming hibiscus bushes.

*I'm thirsty, I'm hungry--I want to go home.*

Hardly had the thought occurred to me, than Ana emerges from the house, walks over to her sister and, as when she arrived, the hugging, kissing, waving, calls and laughter starts all over again.

The sister accompanies Ana to the door and the children to the stairs. They sit there in a row, which looks funny. Seven children of different skin and hair colours. From bright white coffee to the darkest Garifuna black. The hair ranges from frizzy to smooth, from brown to bluish/black.

The suspicion arises that the sisters are the mothers of these children, but that the children have different fathers, which is common in Belize and leads to the most interesting patchwork families. Since it is, anyway, usually left up to the mothers, aunts or grandmothers to raise the children, they still end up growing up in big, happy families. They lack for nothing.

The last one of the children who hugs and kisses Ana particularly warmly, resembles her remarkably. *Aha.*

With rapid steps, Ana walks down the road, back to the bus stop, without discovering her stalker — me. At the bus stop, she enters the phone booth without hesitation, dialling a number from a piece of paper, then speaks excitedly into the phone and leaves the phone booth again when the bus shows up at the end of the road. She is the first in line, hidden by about six or seven people. So I, unnoticed by her, can enter the phone booth, pick up the handset and push the redial button.

"Jonson, state police Belize, San Pedro branch."

Relieved, I hang up the handset and hurry to board the bus.

Now, I know that, finally, the state police has arrived at the resort and is taking the matter into their own hands

My goodness, is *that* a relief!

# Attack from the dark

The closer I get to San Pedro, the queasier the gut feeling in my stomach becomes. But this has absolutely nothing to do with thirst or hunger.

I can vividly imagine how Alex will blow up when he finds out that I had dressed up and followed Ana – all the way to Belmopan.

I can already hear his *"Sandra Sassi"* ringing in my ears.

I must get him to break this habit soon, anyway. He cannot abuse my nice name as a swearword! Maybe I'll try to get back at him in kind?

Alex Tanner! How would that sound? I have to sigh. Certainly, it will not matter all that much to him.

Oh well, today I really exaggerated...I know this myself.

But I have found out that Sabine is at Ana's...I'm quite sure of this...and I have learned that Ana has informed Jonson at the state police. However, is this enough to be considered justification for my trip?

Just as we drive up to the bus stop in San Pedro, I spot Sandy again...disappearing between the houses with a bowl in her hands.

So, little Cleo will get some goodies again today.

And swiftly, I have the thought running through my head that I could speak to Sandy once again — about Duky and Hal Morgan, both of whom have no money, but ambitious plans for their future. Plans one could maybe realize with lucrative additional incomes. For example, with an additional income from drug dealing.

Sandy can perhaps tell me some more about this and I have every confidence in her.

And, moreover, I would still have an additional result to show to Alex. Beside some shrubs, I am waiting until Ana has disappeared on the way to her house. Then, I rush to follow behind Sandy. It is already dusk. In the tropics, darkness falls very fast. I hasten my steps. Suddenly, I hear steps behind me. However, as I look about me, I cannot see anyone. The uncomfortable feeling of being pursued, however, remains. My heart is pounding and my breath is racing. I stay in the shade of the trees and listen, concentrating. Wasn't there a noise, just now? A weak shuffle? Steps? I press myself tightly against the tree trunk and clamp my hands around it. There are no more people on the street, everybody seems to be at home. That was why I had heard the individual steps, because it is otherwise very quiet. But if anyone has been following me, he would have to have gone far in the meantime. I hardly dare to breathe and feel helpless. Why, oh why must I always act on such stupid ideas...over and over again...instead of sitting comfortably on the boat, side by side with Alex, enjoying a fine drink and life in general.

Enjoying life? My own — yes! And what about that of Sabine?

No, I justify things to myself, I cannot possibly be quietly squatting in a corner and simply enjoying my life, while the girl is being pursued or may even be getting killed...*precisely*.

But here, I cannot do anything no more. I abandon the idea of a conversation with Sandy. For today, I must give up. Somehow, I am so relieved about that.

Coward, I scold myself, you are such a coward...

It has already gotten dark in the meantime — a darkness still having weak differences between black and slightly less black, and drawing fine contours of trees and bushes. So, I pause behind the tree for one more moment and listen into the dark, extremely intently. Nothing.

A feeble wind ruffles the leaves of the tree, a few birds, preparing for the night, cheep in the branches. And somewhere, a dog is barking.

Now, I dare to lean forward — and rebound at once, frightened. A black, horrific shape rises up like a mountain in front of me and blocks my path. Briefly, I squeal...and then find myself staring into a menacing face.

The mighty black head with monstrous, matted hair falling down onto the broad shoulders at the sides – rises up before me. The only bright flashes are the white eyeballs in this otherwise black face. Below it is a colossal, naked chest in oversize bulges above the black pants. Tattooed across the chest, there is a yellow flash of lightning. The man seizes me by the arm and holds me tight with an iron grip. A long moment...half an eternity...we stare at each other, two people with nothing in common.

Helplessness in the face of power.

Weakness in the face of force.

David against Goliath.

But David was able to defend himself. I encourage myself, swing out with my knee and lash out against the block of flesh with all the force of which I am capable, and smack against his manhood. A hoarse groaning emerges from the depths of the belly, the flash of lightning twitches across the chest, and the clamp on my arm releases. I seize this moment, slip around the tree through the bushes and race off as if chased by the devil.

Unfortunately, I run in the wrong direction.

Presently, I know this is not the way to the saving dinghy. But I cannot turn back. I would have to pass

Goliath again. And my legs just keep on running, anyway. My lungs are pumping like mad and, quietly, I pray for help, for something to hide behind, for anyone to protect me.

Now, I have no more notion of where I am. Only when a few huts appear between the trees, do I notice that I must have reached the village in an arc. A warm light coming from a back door welcomes me, a lean woman is sitting on the stairs leading to the garden, smoking. She looks towards me quietly and moves aside a bit. Emitting a loud groan, I sink down on the wooden stairs. I need say nothing. The woman with the long, plaited hair looks me in the face, then questioningly into the darkness, and when I nod fearfully, she gets up, takes me by the hand and walks into the house with me.

A bulky old man and two young girls are sitting around a massive wooden table, they have the same long hair, pretty face and shining eyes as the woman from the stairs — their mother. The three at the table have plates with rice and fish in front of them and are hungrily shovelling in the food. The old man looks up only briefly and then continues spooning the food in, steadily and calmly. Both girls jump up and look at me, curiously. They are very pretty, with their smooth, dark skin, the full curved lips, the deep black hair, which is styled like that of the mother, in many, narrow braids. These are two younger, spitting images of their mother — twins.

Presently, I sense that these are nice people and I feel relieved. With a few words, I explain my dilemma and I wisely pass over my spying. A stroll...that was what I had been doing before I lost my way. I am very ashamed for lying to these decent people, but I think it's maybe better not to tell them everything.

Jilly and Pat, the twins, immediately offer to take me back to the dinghy at the shore... I am only too glad to accept. But I want to know from the mother whether this would not be too dangerous for the girls.

"Oh what," she makes a dismissive gesture and points to the old man at the table. "Our grandpa," she says, "was the mayor here for a long time...a person in authority. Nobody would dare touch his granddaughters."

Let's hope, I think, since we are hoping very much these days.

Whether a former mayor is also a person in authority for common criminals? Whether, sometimes, the respect might not be slightly displaced?

In any case, there is nothing else left for me to do than trust these nice people and I go on my way, together with Jilly and Pat.

The twins babble openly about their school and what they would like to be when they grow up. Jilly wants to be a teacher and Pat wants to study marine biology.

"Will this be easy? I mean, studying and all that?" I ask, thinking of the problems of Ana's nephews.

"Sure. Studying in Belize is paid for by the government..."

"... you only have to do well enough at school."

"We are."

"And origin or religion make no difference?"

I do not even want to mention the skin colour...

"Not even whether we are white or black or whatever. We are citizens of Belize – that's enough."

Two great girls, with their feet firmly planted on the ground. The future of Belize is indeed secure with such fine people.

Ashore, they help me to push the dinghy into the water, turn down all invitations to have a drink and depart, laughing and signing.

So, I return to the sailboat, without anyone bothering me.

# Everything is so difficult

There is a hotel powerboat moored at our rail. Alex is sitting at our small table in the cockpit with Duky and two pretty Englishwomen – two really beautiful women — and is playing the gallant host. They all laugh, joke and have fun. Alex, too, is laughing and flirting, and now I'm jealous. And yet, I know, there is nothing there. It is only Alex's revenge because I acted so arbitrarily once more, had simply just run off and, throughout the day, and have been snooping around somewhere. So, he simply got himself a few guests on the boat, in order to prove to me that he also gets along fine on his own, with other people, for example with two very pretty Englishwomen.

He didn't worry at all? Didn't wonder where I was, or even search for me? I had been gone way too long, really. But he couldn't have guessed that I was in danger — nevertheless! A little searching or concern would not have done any harm. Only a little.

I'm quite offended. I welcome Duky cordially, the two English ladies less cordially and scarcely pay any attention to Alex. "I'll get something to nibble on," and then, I disappear into the boat cabin.

Alex follows directly behind, because he has to have a word with me and he wants to do that, I think, as long as his anger is still fresh. No trace of concern, no fear for me — only simple annoyance.

"What were you thinking," he presses out between tight lips, "you were imagining things again and then you simply take off!"

"Alex listen, it was not *simply* and I had not just imagined it."

"Come on, Sandra, I know about your gut feelings and intuitions!"

"And? Wasn't I mostly right? The last time?"

"Hm…"

I expect no answer and continue: "Look, Alex, I don't want to discuss that now, when you have guests, but I need to talk to you later…"

My nerves are strained. This disaster is eating away at my strength. Alex would not be my good Alex, however, if his rage were not already half gone.

"O.k. later," he says and disappears again with the pretty ladies.

I quickly equip a wooden cutting board with ham, tomato slices, cheese cubes and slices of bread and hand it through to the cockpit. Drinks are already abundantly present up above.

Now, I hop under the shower, rinse off my sweat, road dust, and the bad feelings, put on fresh stuff and arrive just in time to say goodbye to the guests.

With a cup of tea, I sit down next to Alex in the cockpit.

The humidity of the day had continued until the evening, but now a light breeze moderates the heat. I am feeling as good as can be, probably, with all that fear for and worry about Sabine.

"Alex," I begin, "I'm so tired and disappointed. So disappointed that we don't know how Sabine is at all."

"You must not get personally involved, yourself, in such a way, we have the state police for that now. Mister Jonson. I swam to the shore today — for lack of dinghy — to speak with him."

"And? Did you tell him about our observations in the small bay?"

Alex hesitates, "No...not yet."

"Don't you trust Jonson?"

"Yes, he is a capable young man. An excellent expert... trustworthy, determined. But I mean, we don't know who was there at the bay yet. We may put ourselves in danger, if we spread our knowledge."

"Hm... Yes, I understand that. And, would you like to know how I found out about Jonson? That he is at the resort now?"

"Hm..."

"I admit, I have really exaggerated a little today with... well...the snooping around. But I have so many questions and I cannot just sit around and do nothing."

"But you just ran off. Without thinking."

He wants to say the familiar lines again but I pre-empt him, "I know, my feet often respond faster than my brain. But my gut feeling is clearly working better than my mind."

"If only you could sometimes coordinate this better!"

"Hm...that is just how it is."

Then, I tell him about my trip to Belmopan, that Ana had called Jonson and that I found out by using the redial button. That she probably did that because she has Sabine with her. And, out of San Pedro..."

"Oh Sandra..."

"... she had not dared to call out of San Pedro."

"You cannot know that, really!"

"I'm saying — assume, suspect! If I knew, I would not have to spy."

I list my assumptions:

That I saw someone with Ana at the window, someone slender.

That I am almost sure that Sabine is with Ana.

"Almost. You know that only almost, Ana knows where Biene is, but maybe she's not with her at the house, or is no longer with her."

"Hmm, Yes."

I continue to report that there were men in the village, sneaking around...I almost wanted to say, "threatening people." But that is something I do not have to tell Alex for now. Therefore, I continue: "why do we never see the police at all properly conducting searches or questioning people? For example, going around with boats to the surrounding islands? Why do the policemen creep around everywhere, but a really serious hearing — for example, at the hotel — has not yet taken place? Do they still assume there was an accident, and why? If this is a kidnapping, why has nobody called for the ransom yet?"

Alex tries to calm me down. "If you are thinking that Sabine is with Ana, why did the state police not fetch her today, immediately after Ana's telephone call?"

"I don't know that."

"You can't know everything. Or rather, you cannot know how the questions must be asked. Perhaps the kidnappers have already been in touch, and the police are still keeping this secret. Or, if Sabine is with Ana, the police could not get her yet, because...oh, I don't know, either." My clever Alex has a thousand theories.

"They are not going to tell us everything they do and know."

I give this some thought, calming down a little. "Yes, that could be...but I'm not sure, everything seems so funny to me. So unprofessional." Shivering, I wrap my arms around myself. I'm cold all of a sudden.

"The state police, I mean Jonson with his troop, only arrived this afternoon. Give them some time..."

"We don't have time. Sabine has no time!"

"What do you suggest we do?"

"We go to the resort again tomorrow and talk to Jonson. I would also like to meet this Jonson. And we tell him everything we know. What we saw in the small bay and on Cay Caulker."

Alex gets up energetically, "...but enough of the talking for now. Now, we shall eat, if the greatest of all detectives would find it possible at all to put something together for her hungry husband."

Alex looks me in the face and probably realizes that I'm still not really there, but that I am mentally floating away somewhere.

"So, then just don't," he sighs, resigning himself to his fate, walks into the kitchen and begins to conjure something up for himself.

# The conversation with Jonson of the state police

We encounter Jonson in his office at the resort.

At once, I understand that this man knows his craft. He is not in vain Chief of the State Special Commission for drug-related crimes, although he has barely passed his fortieth year.

The instructions he gives to his subordinates are clear and precise. He speaks calmly and reasonably, remains down to earth as he does so and, nevertheless, expects that his words are being heard and his orders are obeyed. He exudes strength.

His dark face, which is the image of Africa in its purest, most raw form, makes me think of the suffering of his black ancestors, who had once been deported here. When you look into the black eyes...I deem that I can hear muffled sounds of bush drums and of an elephant ROAR.

His immaculate shirt, grey pants and the gold watch on his wrist immediately bring me back into the here and now. His precise orders, which he barks into the telephone receiver, the fast hand movements, which he performs above the laptop, and the scanty, but extremely precise instructions he throws at his people — all this gives me the impression that I am somewhere in a high-rise office in London, New York or Zurich.

Jonson is tall and his skin is jet black — a very handsome man. His high forehead, prominent nose and curved, broad lips, which are often drawn into a smile that is quick to come, making him a pleasant chap.

He pulls out two chairs for us and then sits down on his, behind Hal Morgan's desk that he has summarily annexed and declared his "Office."

"Already for some months," he begins to say calmly, "I have had my eye on a drug pusher gang, suspected to have many followers in the region, and I think they are trafficking drugs through Belize to Mexico and the United States. As soon as I heard of the strange disappearance of two tourists, I put two and two together, made a connection with some of the other information that has piled up on my desk lately, and figured out what might be going on here."

He arranges some papers and continues, "...the anonymous telephone call..." while casting a stern look at Alex, "alarmed me and immediately prompted me to relocate my office here to San Pedro."

"We are very happy about this," Alex interjects. "We, my wife Sandra and I, are out at anchor with our sailboat. We've, well, Sandra, has seen a lot."

Alex looks at me, as though to give me the cue.

"Tell him, Alex, you're better — in English."

So Alex informs Jonson about what is happening in the small bay, about the girls and the men pursuing them. And that one of them was wearing a police uniform.

Jonson leans forward and listens intently. His whole body posture, his stance, signal undivided attention.

"Then this sleek motor yacht with the American flag arrived at the bay on Cay Caulker. We...I mean, Sandra... observed how crates were being loaded at night and that there were also men on the shore. Of these, again, two policemen!"

"Why didn't I learn about that yesterday?" Jonson looks stern.

I start off, "We...," clearing my throat, "we didn't know whether we could trust you."

"I understand...the police uniforms."

I hand the roll with photo negatives over to Jonson, containing the pictures that I shot at Cay Caulker and that we had still not developed yet. "That is something one cannot do here, only in Belize downtown, the capital, and we had not gotten there yet. We would also never have dared to entrust these to a stranger."

Jonson nods. He takes the negative roll over to one of his people, with a brief order, and then sits down with us again.

"I have done these at Cay Caulker, too," I explain, and hand Jonson the sketch of the American boat crew. Again, Jonson nods politely, he looks at the sketch briefly and sets it aside.

Alex now also reports what I had overheard in the smoke-filled police station...that I had followed Ana and found out that she had just got off the phone to him, Jonson, which, in our opinion, had been the reason for her trip to Belmopan. Jonson just looks at me briefly and nods.

Alex tells him nothing about my suspicion that Sabine could be with Ana. I am just about to inhale, catch a mouthful of air, and open my mouth to speak and tell him precisely that, but then I stop. Well, it is a bit vague, after all. Perhaps she's really hidden somewhere else. And maybe Ana had told Jonson something about that, in any case...and then he knows about it already.

At the end of the report, the detective looks at me in silence for a long time, and then he says, "I suppose you know that you have put yourself in great danger. At least, you have been really able to help us. But we will now take it from here! You keep still and..."

"I shall vouch for this!" Alex says grimly.

Jonson smiles mischievously, and I resent this a great deal. It is another one of those male conspiracies. Male bonding, argh!

Then, once again, we have to describe everything precisely, with dates, times and locations:

The men, who had chased after Biene and Kati in the small bay.

The motor yacht, the people on it, the small boats, which arrived at night, in order to bring the crates, the policemen there on the beach.

What I had heard at the police station, and the description of these men.

Above all, Ashton interests him.

And everything that revolves around Ana and the bar.

Jonson draws all the information onto a map of Belize.

Then he warns us — me — again: "These men are very dangerous, they spare nothing and nobody."

"I have…," I say, "a couple of...well, suspicions…Alex, what is *Verdacht* in English? Help me out here."

"I do not believe that Mr. Jonson cares."

"Tell him anyway!"

He just refuses, gets up, says goodbye to Jonson and leaves. I lean over Jonson's desk and jot down a few names and notes on a piece of paper. Then I hand the note to him with the following words, in my horrible English: "this people, I think … sorry."

Hopefully, Jonson can do something with these.

He stares at the few names and comments, then to my face, and slowly nods his head.

Why do I only interpret the questioning look in his black eyes as mistrust? Why do I feel that he will not even consider the note?

I smile at him and hurry after Alex.

On looking back, I see, however, that Jonson is studying the note, frowning.

On the note, I had written:

1. Mel David, the chief of the village police, has expensive wife, expensive house. Could have been policeman in the small bay.

2. Bartender Duky has whispered with Mel David? Needs money for high-flying bar plans?

3. Hotel manager, Hal Morgan, from where money for all the conversion work? (Hotel is never fully booked.)

Bullish, black chap, who threatens people in the village.

I'm very curious what our efficient Jonson will make of all this.

Alex is waiting for me outside the police station, takes me by the hand and decides, "Today, *you* will come for a stroll with *me*."

"Village? *Again?*"

He grins and counters: "You had always wanted to see downtown Belize, right?"

This is a great idea...I'm in.

Our dinghy takes us to the dock of the speedboat, where we board for Belize City.

The speedboat is already crammed tight with people. They are of the usual composition found at Ambergris Cay. So, you can see brown and black skin colours of all imaginable shades. We are the only white people, *gringos*, there.

So, we squeeze in between fat women with children on their laps, who move aside for us a little, and between men smoking thin cigarettes.

We are under siege with a thousand questions, above all me — from the women.

"From where?" this is always the first question, then *what, why, how*.

When the *"how"* comes, I notice that the women know exactly who we are, that we are travelling and living on the sailboat. It is for sure the only one that has been cruising about in the area for three weeks and is at anchor outside San Pedro, and therefore, everyone knows about us, completely and exactly down to the point. And in the village, we have already met some of the people there in any case.

The "how" is always also a question regarding money. Whether we are rich, they ask, and how much such a boat as ours would cost.

Most of the questions, however, concern our family at home, how many children, grandchildren, and how can they get along without us, why we ever went away.

This is something I can understand well...these women are loyal family people, who would never leave their loved ones behind. Only the men, who bounce from one family to the other, depending on which woman they belong to at the time. But that we would leave our families behind, in order to see the world, this is beyond the scope of their horizons.

"We like it here, we want to see that too."

That, again, the old woman beside me can understand. She rocks her grandchild on her knees and looks at her with love. Then she murmurs, "...but to go away, therefore? Sorry, but...I think..."

*And you, Sandra*, I think, *what will you do once you have a grandchild or two? Oh what, naturally, I shall keep on sailing with Alex.* I have not yet seen enough of this world by a long way. And the grandbaby, I can visit him or her at times. Or the grandchild can visit us.

At Belize City, as soon as our speedboat has moored, the crowding starts again. Everyone wants to get off immediately. That cannot be done very fast however, the gate is narrow and most of the people have a width that can only laboriously be pushed through the passage. Finally, we also leave the boat and dock and go over to the seaside walkway.

"Already... please do not start to run off again, just like that!" Alex seizes me by the arm.

"First, let's see how to get into the city centre and to the market," I stop and take a look around.

"We'll just follow the pack, then we will certainly get to the place," Alex says, always considering things from a practical point of view.

"That is exactly what I wanted to do."

We stroll along the pier, and the smaller, mostly desolate docks, where fishing boats are moored.

At one of the jetties, there are many men, standing there as though nailed to the spot, and they stare down at something, off the end.

We move closer and, at first, do not understand what's going on.

Between the two front posts of a wooden construction, we can see two men through the clear water, floating just beneath the surface.

For God's sake, what are they doing there? *Under Water*!

I can tell from the horrified expressions on the faces of the bystanders that something terrible must have happened. Carefully, I step closer and I can now see that the two men are tied to the poles under water. They are precisely at a height that meant their heads must have been still above the water at first. The rising water of the tide would then have reached their mouths and noses and drowned the helpless men.

What a horrible death.

Spellbound, I stare at the two dead men.

Alex holds me back by my shoulders and his voice whispers in my ear, "Get away from here."

Just as I spin around, I can see a man I know staring at the dead, as I had just done.

Ashton. Ashton, the quiet man from the police station.

Ashton, too, now allows himself to be led away by a colleague. As though in a trance, he walks across the jetty and climbs into a fishing boat.

For us, of course, the trip ends here. Shocked, we return to the speedboat and then to Ambergris.

# A sailboat trembles through the reef

"Unfortunately our time as the sole sailboat in the bay is over..." With a nod, I point in the approximate direction of the reef cut, where I can see a two-mast sailboat heading for the pass. Alex sets aside his cutlery and disappears into the cabin, where he tunes to the emergency channel 16 on the radio.

"You never know," he shouts up to me, "today, there are so many disgustingly short, choppy and steep waves...and maybe they do not know the reef!"

With my obligatory binoculars, I'm already at the rail: "Really not ideal for the poor dears. Better stay on the radio, maybe we need to triage them. Oh drat!"

I notice it at that very same moment. "I believe they may be having genuine difficulties!"

Strained, rigid, I stare at the sailboat at the reef edge. Alex comes up with the appropriate sea chart and says, "You better get on the radio, Sandra! Tell them, how they must first steer towards the village and then towards the point of land, in order to come around the reef correctly."

"Yes, yes, yes," I nod after each sentence and hurry to the radio at the navigation table.

Alex climbs into the dinghy, starts up the engine. He yells back, "...and they must!"

The rest is lost in the wind. But anyway, I know how one has to take this reef cut, I had already guided the *Seeschwalbe* through it several times.

It turns out — as the crew later told us — that they were neither familiar with the reef entry, nor with the disgusting current conditions, and things happen as they must:

I become aware of a dreadful rumbling and scratching at my navigation table, and realise they have taken the curve around the sharp reef corner too tight. Since they also do not seem to care about the radio, I hurry into the cockpit and I can see, through the binoculars, that they are really stuck on an edge of the reef. I also see how Alex shouts something through the funnel he has shaped with his hands, and quickly pulls himself up on the rail from the dinghy, tethering our dinghy on a bollard.

Already, he is standing on the strange deck, looking around.

He shouts commands, pulls up the sails and goes to the controls. Somehow, I have the feeling that the two shocked sailors don't really react as Alex would like them to. The next gust of wind, however, heels the boat over, and by using the engine power, Alex manages to push the ship off the coral.

That is how the *Sunshine*, a beautiful two-mast sailboat, soon comes to lie at anchor beside the *Seeschwalbe* in the sheltered lagoon. The crews of the two sailboats meet on our boat for a late lunch.

But first, the men quickly dive down below the *Sunshine*, in order to examine the damage that the reef edge has caused to the boat's hull. Relieved, Hansi reports that there were only a few scratches, which he himself can fix. He intends to do that at the marina outside Belize City, where there is a crane to lift the boat out of the water. And they would have gone there anyway, soon. They had wanted to leave the *Sunshine* at the marina in any case...a home furlough is imminent.

Alex and Hansi shower off the seawater and sit down at the cockpit table to eat.

"So, you are not going to stay here for long, in San Pedro?"

"A day or two, once we have recovered from the horrors of today."

"However, you managed to get through in one piece."

"Yes, sure. It was funny," Hansi muses, laughing and running his hand through his grey stubble of hair, "suddenly having a stranger on board, barking commands. And in the most precious, beautiful Swiss German, at that! But thanks, eh, and the next meal is on us."

That said, he stuffs my fine, crispy bread into his mouth and keeps spooning in the soup that I had quickly diluted to make enough for four eaters. Now that the guests have had their fill, Hansi tells of the dilemma of his trip here, which started two days ago at Isla Mujeres in Mexico.

"That was a mess up there." He shudders at the mere memory. "Two large American navy vessels of the DEA and... certainly five, or six, of the smaller Mexican man of war ships had been buzzing around, searching for drug smugglers, and making all of us nervous. But, apparently, they had been successful and caught a drug dealer boat. The most incredible rumours of huge quantities of heroin and even dead people were flying around. No-one, of course, knew any precise details. We heard some shots. It was uncomfortable for us and we wanted nothing but out.

"There were five other sailboats anchored at Isla Mujeres. Immediately after the DEA had searched all of us and checked our papers, we decided to sail off. We did not really watch out for the weather, though. A sh...a.. trip that was."

Hansi shakes his head at the bitter memories. Marlies nods in confirmation. "Yes, and being that hell bent on leaving, without checking the weather first...before you know it, you get yourself head on into the next disaster and you end up stuck on the reef."

"Where did the other sailors head for?" Alex wants to know.

"I think all of them went northward. There were yanks, who anyway would have been waiting at Isla Mujeres for a weather window for the trip to the United States. You can imagine that the DEA checked these boats especially thoroughly. The drugs are supposedly being smuggled into the USA, particularly."

"And they were allowed to leave then, after the check?" I ask.

Alex interjects, "They did not have such good weather, either. The Gulf of Mexico is quite a handful in bad weather. I would not want to travel through there for the life of me."

"Hm, yes," Hansi responds, "they preferred to be stuck in bad weather rather than get involved in drug stories. Same as us."

Hansi tells us that the drugs were being trafficked into the USA via Belize and Mexico. They would, supposedly, move tons of heroin every year and everywhere along the coast, there were workers who transported the illegal goods, passed them on and distributed them at the place of destination. Hansi disapprovingly shakes his head: "And before you know it, you are stuck in the middle of this sh…"

Considering his words, I look at Alex. "Do you think that this has anything to do with the disappearance of the two girls? With our drug boat?"

Alex shakes his head. "I think you're seeing ghosts again, Sandra. That would be a mighty coincidence."

"Can you describe the drug boat?" I ask Hansi.

Hansi thinks about it. "We didn't see it up close, it was one of these large motorsailer with a US flag. With five people on it."

I exclaim: "Could fit!"

"You cannot describe the people?" Alex, who always wants to be sure, asks.

"Huh...no. They only arrived around evening time and the whole thing then went on at night. I mean, the only thing I saw was how the police had searched the shore at night. Maybe some of them were able to escape."

"Possibly," Alex opines, "and, in no time, they are on their way again with the drugs."

"And speaking of disappearing, where has good Marlies actually vanished to?" I ask.

We all look down into the boat cabin and see Marlies snoring away comfortably on the bench in the living room — in a deep and blissful sleep.

# Difficult conversation at the resort

I fled the *Seeschwalbe* in the wee hours of morning, in order to escape the prospect of sitting around idly and engaging in constant musing about *why and how*...I am so fed up with all of this.

I have apparently also greatly annoyed Alex with my eternal considerations of what happened — or what might be happening. Now he wants to get rid of me, danger or not.

"That gets us nowhere, Sandra," he finally said, with a resigned expression on his face.

He suggests that I should hang out at the resort...or something. I should not snoop around but should swim like a normal guest, or go strolling, or have a cup of coffee. He still wants to do a few repairs to the boat and would not be able to come along.

So, I grab my bathing suit and a book, put them in my beach bag and get out of his way.

I drive past the *Sunshine* with the dinghy, in order to see whether Marlies or Hansi need something, or whether someone would like to come along to the resort. Nothing seems to move about on the boat. The trip yesterday must have really stressed both of them out. So, I let them sleep and go on to the resort on my own.

The golden sun shines down warmly from a blue sky, the lagoon lies before me, calm and turquoise, and the hibiscus flowers in the park sparkle in competition with the water. A few hotel guests are strolling across the cleanly swept paths, and children are frolicking about on the beach.

Their laughter floats all the way up to me. I am sitting on the terrace with a cup of coffee and am enjoying the humid, but today, for once, not scorching air. It is clearly more pleasant this way.

"May I sit with you?"

The South German accent makes me listen up attentively.

"Jonson told me that you knew Kati?"

An elegant woman looks at me quizzically, and I can immediately see who I have in front of me. Kati's mum. The similarity is striking.

The same thin hair, the same fine-drawn mouth and even the calm, quiet voice is the voice of Kati.

"You are welcome to, Mrs. Meusch. Yes, we knew…the girls. It…I'm so sorry…about Kati."

Mrs. Meusch, who had travelled from Germany last night, with her husband and Biene's parents, told me about Katharina – her dead child.

The woman looks exhausted. She is plucking at her thin fingers with painted fingernails and repeatedly running them through what is bound to have previously been a well-groomed hairstyle on her head. She also has silvery hair, just like her daughter Katharina, only that hers has been trimmed chin-length by a specialist, has a soft perm, curls interspersed with bright streaks. Now, however the perm's curls are in disarray and are hanging into her eyes. Her delicate face is very pale and the blue eyes are clouded with grief.

"You should lie down a little."

But she shakes her head, "I can't, it's good for me to talk to someone."

"How did you get here soon, I mean…?"

."..It was terrible…we got this message…I was unable to think straight anymore." But my lady housekeeper, Eveline, she called…and had acted very smart…called my husband and the Kellers, Sabine's parents. She packed our bags and Guido Keller, Biene's dad, organised everything."

It's all a little confusing but I understand.

Now, she tells me about Kati. About a little, cute girl from the small town of Stockach, where she went to school with her girlfriend Sabine, who was always around and who helped Kati to transform her house in Stockach into a madhouse. Except for when the two of them were in the progress of turning the home of Sabine upside down instead. Happy go lucky Biene had done her rather shy child a lot of good. She continues to report how the two girls grew up as though they were sisters. How they used to play together, study together and fell in love with the same guys, had a crush on the same stars. How, at last, they had graduated together from high school, for which they had been given this trip to Belize as a reward. She tells of the quiet town where they used to live, the beautiful house with the big garden, which connects to the garden of the Kellers, Sabine's parents.

She jumps back and forth from one thought to another, and between experiences, images and impressions.

Kati…used to be all she had. How this woman must hurt to have lost her beloved, only child.

Now, the mother pauses and asks quietly, "Where might Sabine be?"

She blows her nose and dabs the tissue over her swollen eyes. Quietly, she continues, "The girls were accustomed to going out by themselves, even in the evening. They knew the dangers and respected the boundaries set for them. Even on vacation…they had travelled alone already twice before."

Her voice grows ever quieter.

Well, it is a good thing I always have clean tissues on me, one of which I put into her hand. Then, I tell her, "We met Biene and Kati, they seemed to us to be two independent and sensible girls. They have certainly not recklessly put themselves in danger, and for sure they are…"

Gee, that sounds contrived!

But how can you even try to comfort a mother who has just learned that her daughter has been brutally murdered? And how one can make her understand that it is not her or the girls themselves who are to blame for the crime?

"We had met the two of them on the beach and they were with us on the sail boat." I point to the bay, where you can just about still see our boat gleaming through the palm trees in the sun, down at the promontory.

"We are so sorry, it's terrible."

Mrs. Meusch looks me in the eye, "I heard you were looking for the girls. Mr. Jonson said that you had found out something yourself?"

"Yes. We were afraid for the girls and had searched the coast as good as we could from our yacht but, unfortunately…" I interject awkwardly, "we were unable to do anything."

"Yes, I know. Nobody… was able to do anything."

"What are you going to do now?"

"My husband is with Jonson and with Biene's parents. They are discussing the…repatriation of our child. Sabine's parents will stay behind here…my God, these poor people. To not even know anything at all about what is going on with your own child."

I keep looking at this woman in awe…she, who, in the midst of her own great suffering, is thinking about the grief of the other girl's parents.

Mrs. Meusch suddenly gets up and squeezes my hand, "I should probably go find my husband now…"

Lost for words, I remain behind and watch the unfortunate woman walk off.

# A fax brings joy

After I left Mrs. Meusch and the resort, it helps me to take a walk into the village — not only to clear my head but also to pick up a long fax from Lisa.

She has three pieces of good news for me, her mum.

She will come to see us during her holidays, sometime in April or May.

They are looking for a new flat, because they are going to get married.

And my child is pregnant! I am going to be a grandma!

The first bit of news is great, I haven't seen Lisa in such a long time, after all.

The joy at the second news is dimmed a bit by Lisa, because she states that the wedding would be small, without family and pomp. Pity!

However, about the third bit of news, my joy is enormous. I will be a grandma!

Exhilarated, I return to our boat, waving the fax from afar for Alex to see.

He helps me tie up the dinghy and says, "No need to ask whether you got good news. Your eyes are sparkling like poinsettias…blue ones."

Keenly, I tell him the good news.

He hugs me. "So, your kid will come to see you during the holidays, although your child is going to have a child herself."

"My child is, after all, already more than thirty years old. And yes, they will come here. But, certainly, my child is always my child. And I am suffering and am glad for every bit of news."

"And that you are not going to be there at the wedding, is that joy or pain?"

Haltingly, I respond, "Not exactly pain...but regret, maybe?"

Alex looks me in the eye. He can understand that I would have wanted to be there at Lisa's wedding. Him, too. Although Lisa is not his daughter, he likes her a lot and has adopted her ... somehow... in his heart.

"Listen, though I know it's not the same, we will post-celebrate the wedding when they are here, whether they want to or not. All right?"

"That's fine, Alex, after all, what do they think they are doing, having a wedding without parents. And on the boat, they cannot get away from us, right?"

"They will not have a say in it, once you have set your mind on something, right?"

Alex hugs me tight, "But you are right. We shall celebrate at the restaurant *Seeschwalbe*, like every day. Namely, there will be crawfish or fish — same as almost every day. They will hardly notice that it is a wedding reception and you, nevertheless, will get your will."

"Aha," I snap at him and pry myself loose from his arms

"Oh, I see, this is what you want to do? Just watch out that it won't be your wedding being celebrated without you noticing."

Alex smirks. "That would still be missing, to come under the thumb."

"Under the thumb! Mine?" I exclaim.

He looks at me distrustfully from the side, "As if I wouldn't now and again have the feeling sometimes or the suspicion — there is coming under the thumb without marriage?"

"Feeling! Suspicion! Now you are starting as well!"

In my comfortable corner, I read through the fax again. Paper and pen for the answer are ready by my side.

Smiling, I read the short remark Lisa made because of the search for accommodation. She wrote, "an apartment, both of us would like."

For a long time, I have known that Lisa and Georg like each other very much, but nevertheless, may not want or be able to live together. And I also know where the problem lies.

Georg states he cannot live in an overheated, stuffy cocoon together with Lisa and Lisa says that she is freezing as soon as she enters Georg's bare designer flat.

What, for Lisa, is the perfect example of living comfort, to Georg, is sheer horror. The differences are about Lisa's comfortable home in the middle of Lucerne near the Museggtürmen, Nine Towers – compared to Georg's bare expensive penthouse flat, full of metallic uneasiness, in an apartment block in Schönbühl centre in the same town.

Lisa's old heavy pieces of furniture and the portly, comfortable couch, versus Georg's bed in the bare cubicle bedroom and the clattering metal pieces of furniture.

It is a quarrel about lifestyle, a fight for the most basic attitudes and views. It is a cold war fought with affectionate taunts and gentle allegations. But still a dispute, where nobody wants to give an inch.

Alex and I had already had several discussions on this. I had once said: "If Georg is as stubborn as my pigheaded daughter…"

"She has got that from you!" he countered.

"... then I see gloomy times ahead for this relationship."

But to this day, at least it has lasted. I know that even if, in all other everyday things, these two are wonderfully in agreement, Georg would never want to live in a chunk house, as he calls it. Just as Lisa is not able to stand being in his desolate fridge-like dwelling.

And now, now everything is completely different.

A child is on the way and suddenly, they are searching for a new flat they both like.

"How a child not yet born can already turn the life of his parents upside down."

Swiftly, I climb into the boat, then into the front cabin and check on blankets and cushions. Do I have enough covers for everybody? Are they tidy? Do they smell stale? Do I need to wash everything? Buy some more?

My good skipper Alex is standing in the drawing room and shakes his head "You are not possibly already starting to make up the beds! They won't be here for another couple of weeks! I understand your joy concerning the visit of your child...but this is...this is..."

"Just let me do my thing, Alex. We once agreed that I would be responsible for household and shopping. You keep worrying about the boat and such stuff."

I open all the boxes and shafts, count towels, cushions and covers and pick up a piece of paper on which I check everything. Alex watches me for a while, and then he leaves, still shaking his head. The remark "impossible obsession", which I pick up as he walks off, really gets me going.

"Alex, listen...just consider this. The bed sheets I might still need, perhaps Lisa can bring them for me from Switzerland. Together with all the other things I would like to have, anyway. Cheese, soup cubes..."

"But now, already!" Alex exclaims, unnerved.

Unimpressed, I continue, "...Baking mixture, risotto rice and my favourite kind of chocolate. She still needs time to buy everything and can only take these things along if she flies via the USA, where 72 kilograms of luggage are permitted per person. Therefore she must know which flight she needs to book...on time..."

"That reminds me," Alex says and no longer pulls an irritated face, "she could then also bring me the missing engine filters and a fan belt..."

"Aha... and that she must still order on time, that must also still be delivered, and also ..."

Alex laughs and his left eyebrow shoots upwards: "I think we will put everything together and will send Lisa the list... namely now...immediately."

# Luxury yacht with drawbacks

In the cockpit of the *Sunshine*, we are feeling good and enjoying being spoilt by Hansi and Marlies. The *Sunshine* is a stately boat, its generous interior design puts our little *Seeschwalbe* to shame. Nevertheless, I would not swap her, because I love the little *Seeschwalbe* precisely because of its handy smallness. And the reduced workload involved — because of this more confined space.

Thus, our smaller ship also has lighter sails, more manageable anchors and winches, and above all, less surface area for painting, cleaning and renewing. The lack of sufficient space for all kinds of electrical equipment and machinery does not bother us, for everything of importance for navigation and seaworthiness, for all manoeuvres and the sailing, and for water supply and electricity supply is present in good quality.

Small but fine, we always say.

Now, nevertheless, we enjoy without envy the chill drink with the jangling ice cubes from the freezer and the appetizing cheese morsels from the microwave. I lean back comfortably, "This is a fantastic atmosphere all around."

The evening sun floats over the island like a gigantic balloon and dips the beach the water and the sky into a dream vision of red and gold

In a kitschy way, it is, however, delightful!

Everything is flooded with gold. Every metal piece in the ship flashes as though made of pure gold and even the four faces at the table have a golden glow to them.

"The maiden with the golden hair," Alex jokes and really, my — blondish from the sun, but otherwise greyish — white mop of hair looks like spun gold in the setting sun.

Only this colour does not agree at all with the dishes on the plates that Marlies now puts before us. The steaks look like brown-grey modelling clay, the fine beans seem to have wilted and the crisply roasted potatoes have a touch of putrefaction colour. Besides, everything is cooked delicately and arranged tastefully on fine porcelain.

"Where can you find these splendid steaks and the fine little beans in this wild region?" I think of my eternal search for reasonably edible meat and fresh vegetables

"And," Alex throws in, "from which cellar does this noble wine come. I must say…"

Marlies laughs. "For the food I simply open my well-stocked freezer and…the wine we have from our cellar. In our bilge, there are about 200 bottles of wine, well packed still from home."

Hansi seems to me to be a bit of a braggart. He lists the fine varieties he has stashed away, mentions the noble names, and at last, even the prices.

We enjoy the fine evening meal that Marlies has prepared in her great kitchen on the 18 metre boat. And this kitchen really offers everything, as I can assess myself:

Respectively one refrigerator and freezer, full of fresh produce, and a vegetable cabinet, where the green stuff remains green and fresh at a gentle $8°+$ temperature, and besides, there are generous working surfaces. There are two sinks and a rack with drainage gutter manufactured specifically for the cleaning of fish or vegetables. A monstrous coffeemaker and a permanently mounted food processor for Kneading, mixing, chopping and pureeing are within handy reach. On a practical sliding board, I see different devices with amazement, such as an egg boiler, toaster, an electric can opener and a small hand blender. Of course, the kitchen also has a microwave, oven with grill and — yes, really, installed underneath the worktop, there is a washer and dryer.

And anything and everything is electric! Where does one get all this electricity from on the *Sunshine*? We must always be a little stingy on our *Seeschwalbe,* with power from our solar panels and the wind generator. And, nevertheless, we need only one fraction of what this boat needs, with all its electric luxury.

I just want to ask a relevant question when Marlies presses a red button and, already, a motor starts humming.

"This is our generator, which I need for the coffeemaker," Marlies answers in response to my questioning look.

"Of course, also while cooking, baking and washing and then, twice a day, for one hour in general for anything else — it is a bit annoying, I know, but luxury comes at a price!"

Indeed, I think quietly, this is tiresome. We join the men for coffee.

"What are your plans for the near future?"

Alex asks the question that is the most common among yachtsmen.

Where from and where to is always important.

"You know, unfortunately we have to go on again. Already tomorrow, we will be off…"

"Should we help you get out from the reef?"

"Oh yes, with pleasure, right away tomorrow morning…"

"…with the first good light."

Finally, we say goodbye and return to our boat. I snuggle up in my corner and Alex gets himself a glass of wine and comes over to the chart table.

"It is more than just a little tiresome, this rumbling generator," I say. I shake my head. "I would rather knead my bread by hand and renounce restocked food awoken from its eternal sleep in the ice."

I loll about in my corner, and suck at my Baileys, my preferential nightcap. "Nevertheless, I have to admit that the food Marlies dished up for us — oh well — was really something special. I cannot compete, of course, with my preserved shredded meat and the salad rescued from the tropical heat."

"Yes, you can" Alex counters, pouring himself yet another glass of wine from the penultimate bottle of his modest stock. "Your food is as good. Think only of all the fine seafood we get from the coral gardens almost daily, precisely because we can't resort to the freezer. And these are as fresh as no frozen steak and no thawed vegetables could ever be. Or, how about your excellent, freshly baked bread? However," he says a little bit wistfully, "the great wine cellar is something I would really like to have."

Nevertheless, he actually looks quite content, my good Alex, sitting there at his chart table, checking something in the sea chart, and now and then taking a sip from his wine glass.

"The wine cellar happens to be part of the luxury yacht, just like the princely cuisine, and the noble furnishings. Hansi and Marlies are rich people. We can't keep up."

I also do not want to, actually. My eyes wander across the well-equipped chart table, where Alex finds everything in reach that he needs for navigation. Content, I look at the small kitchen that, although tiny, is nicely furnished in wood and where I manage to conjure up my fine menus, in each case with a few simple steps. And, once again, I admire the pretty drawing room with its mahogany furniture. Yes, I must say, I wouldn't want any other home.

Then, my thoughts turn from the boat to the surroundings. They deal with much more serious problems than lacking fresh meat or having a badly equipped wine cellar. I sigh sorrowfully.

Alex notices it and asks "Are you still thinking of the washing machine or the microwave?"

Serious, I shake my head. "No, this doesn't really bother me all that much. For all its relief as far as everyday work is concerned, I still wouldn't want it, not at those prices! Breakfast with engine noise instead of bird's twitter, lunch including diesel stench and for the cultivated dinner — would you prefer the sounds of waves lapping or the *Brummbrumm* of an engine?"

"No, Alex, really, I stopped thinking about this a long time ago already. I have a totally different subject floating around my brain."

In detail, I tell him about my meeting at the hotel. "I feel so sorry for Kati's mother and would like to help somehow. But I fear this thing is too big for us. I have a really strong hunch …"

"Hunch!" Alex throws his arms up in the air and he almost knocks over the wine glass. "Sandra! These matters are really too big for us, as you yourself have already said. This is not something with which you should interfere."

Alex gives me a warning look. "And now the police from the city are also here! You don't have to help this Jonson character, really. But what we can do is move our boat closer to the resort?"

"No," I brood further. "We had better remain here with the boat, near the village and the bar. Anyway, I believe that everything is happening right here."

"Now you listen to me, woman! If you resume your nosing around in things that are none of your business, then…"

"Then what?"

"…Then we sail off again to Cay Caulker or even further!"

Now I am sulking a little bit. "I do think that these girls are our business."

"Yes, of course, but…," Alex interjects, "but that doesn't mean you have to help the police with their work, or take it over altogether."

"The police! Ha! Do the work of the village police…ten lucky guesses how this village police does their work, might even be entangled in this whole thing…," I get up and wave my hands about.

"Calm down. First of all, you don't know for certain at all, whether they are entangled in this. Now, secondly, Jonson from the capital is here and he really can't be entangled. And, thirdly…," he says seriously, "…and thirdly, I would prefer not to have to always be afraid for you."

Alex has spoken really urgently. Now, he also gets up, comes towards me and lays his arm around my shoulder. He looks me in the eyes and says, "Why don't you lay your little instincts, feelings and intuitions aside for a chance. It's just that I am scared something could happen to you. You always interfere and some people don't like this at all."

"Yes, Alex, I understand. I'll be careful, l promise!"

Alex sighs.

Resolutely, I exclaim, determined, "And tomorrow, after we have helped Marlies and Hansi get out from the reef pass, I will go to the resort again, in order to speak with the people there. Whether you want to come along or not…now, that is your decision."

In a great hurry, I disappear in the direction of the shower.

With mouth agape, Alex looks after me, then shakes his head and before I have closed the door to the shower, I hear him mutter, "This woman! Well, then, this probably means breakfast, lunch and dinner at the resort again tomorrow. Dammit."

# A sad event

As soon as we have helped Marlies and Hansi, from our safe position on board the dinghy, to navigate through the reef, we return to the beach at the resort.

Along the road outside the resort, there are many people waiting for the coach to take them to the speedboat to Belize City.

The coffin, with poor Kati inside, will fly home in the company of her parents, leaving from Belize City.

We hurry to Jonson's office and he informs us about the latest events. The autopsy on Kati in the pathology lab had been completed quickly. The wounds on her forehead had definitely not originated from contact with the corals, but from a hard object, like for example a pipe or a truncheon. Death is bound to have come fast and the body had been thrown into the sea only after death.

Jonson tells us, "They got everything photographed and logged, tidied up the body of the girl and laid it in a metal travel coffin. Also the countless forms that result from such affairs have been quickly and sensitively dealt with. Now everything is ready and many people would like to accompany Kati to her final flight. I will not come along since…I am not able to get away from here. Maybe Ana will call again."

"Have you always been present here, all that time since the first phone call?" Alex asks, surprised.

"I even spent the night here, beside the phone. On an emergency bed. It is Ana who is our only chance. I have no idea where the girl could be."

"And why don't you simply go to see Ana at the bar?"

"We don't know where Ana has hidden the girl. We don't believe it's in her house. This has already been searched by the village police, anyway. Maybe the girl is at another safe hiding place. We must simply wait until she reports to us again, as she has promised. Also, there is this Marc character at the bar. In what function exactly? As a supervisor? And if so, whose side is he on? We simply don't know enough of the details yet."

Especially clearly, I say over and over again, "But I assume Sabine *is* there."

"We cannot rely on assumptions. It is too dangerous…The crooks are waiting for a movement, a sign from us and immediately they will be there before us. They are everywhere, lying in wait. They cannot afford to allow us to find Sabine. They have to be there before us. Sabine has proof of things we can only make assumptions about."

He silently follows the elaborations of Alex, reporting on the events in the dock in the town. He acknowledges his report with a gesture that shows us that he has prior knowledge of these events. In answer to my question regarding whether this is associated with the drug crime, he says, "It is a typical punishment for traitors."

Now we are ready to go to the airport.

In the hotel coach, I am sitting beside the Alert couple from Hamburg, who tell me how they met the two cheerful girls.

"I really didn't like them at first, though," Mrs. Alert remarks sadly. "They were simply too loud for me, too much of a strain on the nerves…particularly one of them, Sabine. But soon they had me wrapped around their little fingers with their charm. We once had the pleasure of getting each other's make-up and hair done," a wistful smile crosses her lips, "really silly. All three of us looked like zombies. And my make-up case, you should have seen that." Mrs. Alert dabs a tissue over her eyes. "And now Kati is dead. And where might Biene be? I wonder whether she is still alive?" I hold Mrs. Alert's hand.

The oppressive heat in Belize City is gruesome. Two minutes after leaving the air-conditioned coach, our clothes stick to our bodies with sweat.

Inside the air-conditioned airport building, it is more pleasant again.

A large group of mourners has turned out. Kati's parents have arrived from the hotel with Biene's parents. I also see Hal Morgan, the hotel manager, Sandy, the tour guide, and Duky, Marc, the diving teacher, with his colleagues, some German hotel guests, many of the office workers and even quite a few people from the village of San Pedro.

They have assigned a small secondary room to be a chapel substitute, put up a table with a white cloth and draped several chairs around it. Everywhere, luxuriant bouquets with wonderfully luminous tropical blossoms fill the room. On the table, there is a simple wooden cross with the name "Katharina" engraved on it, which will be hung up in the village church later on.

The country vicar delivers a moving sermon. He states that all is God's will, intended as a test and for purification.

Just now, in the arrival lounge of the airport, Kati's mum had stood next to me and said that it had not been at all pleasant to her that so much fuss was being made about all this. She would have preferred a quiet farewell. But now, she notices that the people have a real need to say their goodbyes to Kati. Most had probably come all the way from the village. She noted that the country vicar greeted almost everybody by name.

Because I know that the girls had also been to San Pedro, and I know the open character of the two, I can well imagine that they had got to know some of the villagers.

The priest is an impressive man with a voluminous voice. Just now, he stretches his hands towards heaven and blesses all the bowed heads around him. The people recite prayers and look completely absorbed in their murmured words. Thus, I discover a new side to these people.

Devoutness, religiousness.

I have never been aware of this until now, since I had never gone to church in San Pedro myself.

I had taken a look at the church, of course, in the course of my investigations. If somebody in the village had hidden Sabine, I had thought at first that it would perhaps be the priest. But when I saw the church, consisting, so to speak, of nothing but a humble house, I discarded the thought again. The rectory immediately beside the church was just as modest, and was suited just a little as a hiding place.

Now, that is something I like again about this parish priest, that he lives as poorly as most of his parishioners.

So we listen to the soothing words and the moving song. Then, everybody proceeds onto the landing field, where we watch in silence as Kati's coffin gets swallowed up by the dark, cold throat of the airplane, and finally disappears.

# Will this phone call finally come?

Here we are, sitting with Jonson again, and telling him about Kati's farewell.

Sabine's parents have also taken a seat in the group sitting beside us. Mrs. Keller tells us that Ana definitely knows where Biene is, since she has told them on the phone that she sends greetings to the honey bears. This has been a saying between them since Biene was a small girl. Ana can only really know this from Biene. And her child is in good health, Ana had said, but she is afraid to leave her hiding place because everywhere the wrong people would be snooping around.

But if only she would finally get in touch!

On Jonson's desk, there are maps of San Pedro, the resort and the whole Ambergris peninsula. His people constantly come in and out, he discusses various actions with them and enters everything onto the map. It looks like a war zone.

It is a war; a war against the drug smugglers.

"I am organising a large scale search in the village, in the resort and in the surrounding fishing villages up there, on the border with Mexico, anywhere Sabine could be. So we are on site everywhere, once things start to happen. We are letting the village police search the swamps and the southern bays. By now, this much we know for sure, the girl is not there. We do not want the village police in...," he is interrupted, starts to give his orders and then totally forgets us, it seems.

Quietly, we crouch in our corner and observe the efficient police chief.

All hell seems to have broken loose on Jonson's desk, but Jonson has everything firmly under control.

And it seems to me — he is also in control of his ears, eyes and head.

His orders are clear and concise. He is able to inform the people who come and go in the office precisely and send them exactly to where they are needed. In doing so, he maintains his stoic calm and keeps an overview of everything.

In the middle of this beehive, the phone rings. Tensely, everybody stares at the device and Sabine's parents jump to their feet.

Jonson picks up on the first ring and waves with his hand, making signs that people should leave the room and leave him alone with the phone. Everybody follows his instructions.

We understand that it is not directed at us, and so, we listen to how he patiently answers many questions.

"Yes, it is me, Jonson, on the phone. Don't you recognize my voice?

No, the village police are not there.

Yes, I am coming with *my* people.

I understand.

Yes.

That is precisely how I want to do it.

No.

They will only come out when they see the car.

A Chevy, grey, large, with Belizean number plates.

Yes, the parents will come along.

Yes, the whole road of the resort from you will be blocked.

I am leaving.

Yes, now!

He throws the receiver back on the cradle and picks up his car keys. He specifically nods to Biene's parents and briefly says, "You come with me — and you," with this he nods at Alex and then me, "stay behind."

My nerves are extremely on edge. It is terrible to sit around here and to know something is happening, but not to know what. Alex's face expresses the same huge fear I feel, and he looks at me with eyes in which hope and fear are fighting with each other.

We sit in the restaurant and observe how municipal police officers are running around and then some of them get into the cars and disappear from the resort. At each exit, policemen in the uniforms of the State police are standing around. I cannot see the colours of the village police uniforms anywhere, which is something that calms me down.

There is also a terrible atmosphere of fear and dismay among the guests, as well as hopeful expectation. They know less than Alex and me, but they notice that the situation is moving towards a climax.

My fingers are cramped, I bite my lips, get up, look from the window, go back again, crouch on the edge of the chair and twist my fingers again. Until Alex has had too much. He seizes my hands and looks me in the eyes, imploringly.

"It won't get any better like this. Just sit quietly and breathe deeply."

With all my force, I try to do exactly this, but internally, my nerves vibrate even more and thoughts are racing round in circles.

Less than half an hour later, a stunned Jonson sweeps back into the hotel. Ana is hobbling on his arm, injured and pale.

Crying, Mrs. Keller follows him with her husband, who is scared to death.

Jonson hands Ana and Sabine's parents over to the doctor, who has been present in the resort since this morning. He gives instructions to Hal Morgan that he should have everybody taken to their rooms, and tells a subordinate that he should have guard posts put up and allow nobody into the hotel that he does not know. Then, he immediately leaves again.

It is now evening and a tired Jonson returns again. He orders himself something to eat in his office and then immediately runs there.

Alex and I follow behind.

Jonson sits down at the desk and coordinates the search over the radio and on the phone. He shouts and orders, roars and demands — he is like a raging hurricane.

As soon as he has his food in front of him, he recounts the dreadful events between hastily swallowed bites.

"Sabine was there in Ana's house. But when I stormed into the house, I heard only an absolutely shocked Ana shouting for help. Her head was bleeding nastily and it was impossible to get coherent words out of her, except over and over again just the sentence, 'It was no use, everything was for nothing. The men…!'"

In a hurry he eats a few bites, he seems like a starving man. I see desperation in his face. In his black eyes, the bush drums and the lion's roar have fallen silent.

"We came too late. Sabine's mother ran through the house and then she asked Ana where Sabine was."

But Ana only shook her head, "Upstairs, I don't know … I think she's upstairs. She ran upstairs with the men behind her. Scuffles in her room. Maybe she was hiding up in the whisky cupboard."

"Whisky cupboard?" I throw in questioningly.

"Ana has a secret hiding place, where she keeps her alcoholic drinks."

"And was Sabine there?"

"I don't know, I think so. Then Ana fainted and Mrs. Keller broke down."

Jonson buries his face in his hands. "What did I do wrong?"

"How could these men be in the house in the first place? How did they know...?"

"I assume they were present everywhere, waiting. And when they saw us coming ..."

"Did the men take Sabine?" I ask.

Jonson deliberates, "I do not think they found the girl. Sabine must have managed to escape. You still see people everywhere, looking for her."

The Commissioner grins lopsidedly. "We cannot distinguish them from the regular gawkers. We would need to lock up the entire village."

Gradually, his people arrive back with disappointed faces, report to their boss where they had searched and what they had come up with, and he draws everything on his map.

He draws circles and frantically considers all of Sabine's possible escape routes.

Then he hits the map with his flat hand and groans, "She has got to be there, keep looking. Turn everything upside down in Ana's house and everywhere else. Search behind every bush, turn over every stone. Search every damned metre, all the way to here."

And once again, he sends out the tired men. He sends everybody who arrives away again, with the order not to come back without the girl.

"And bring this Mel David character to me!"

Jonson stands at the window, resigned, and stares, half blind, into the dusk that has now fallen.

"Where are you, child?" he whispers, "where for heaven's sake are you?" Then I ask Jonson, "Might it be possible that Sabine...I mean, our boat?"

Jonson stares at me, but his head of operations interjects straight away, "We had your permission to go on your boat and so we went on the boat — there was no trace of the girl."

"When were you there?"

"Immediately, and there were also no footprints on the beach. And later, we checked again. Here, I have taken down the times for you."

Jonson studies the slip of paper and enters the data in his chart.

Because we cannot help here anymore, I am drawn to our sailing boat. A slight suspicion is gnawing away in my brain. Sabine could still seek shelter on our boat, after hiding out somewhere else. If she has not been found on the mainland up to now, she has maybe swum out there and is lying in wait... among the corals? The rocks? So, I want to go back to the boat. Even though I have seen on Jonson's map that they had also searched in the lagoon by boat. But, however, perhaps...?

"Should I send one of my men along with you?" Jonson asks thoughtfully.

Alex wants to answer, but I pre-empt him, "No, of course not, you need all your men here."

Jonson, reluctantly, gives in. But I point out that the police have searched our boat without finding Sabine. The gangsters have certainly also got wind of this. I explain this to Jonson and he confirms, "Of course, they are precisely informed about everything we've done."

"So," I argue, "no-one has any reason to attack us, or anything else."

Finally, Jonson also accepts this argument and he lets us go. However, maybe my iron determination has also "persuaded" him.

Only Alex cannot really accept it yet. The whole way across the beach to our dinghy, he discusses the question of our safety with me, or the possibility of danger, once we are alone on the sailboat. But, finally, he accepts my arguments. I knew that he would.

What I do not know, however, is that Alex can read my thoughts.

After a short period of consideration, he looks at me quizzically, "You still think it's possible that Sabine could come to help for us, out on the boat?"

"Everything's always possible, even the least likely option. We don't know where the girl has been hidden and when she will dare to come out from that hiding place. In any case, I want to be on the boat. And without guards. Without men who trample around on the boat and whom Biene doesn't know."

# Late Visit

I snuggle up comfortably in my reading corner and try to become engrossed in a crime book. But I can't concentrate at all on what's written, because — over and over again — my thoughts circle around Sabine and the whole gigantic mix-up.

"How is this going to end? Is Sabine even still alive?"

"What do you mean?" Alex lifts up one earphone a bit. "What did you say?"

"Oh, only thinking out aloud, Alex."

Concentrating, I try to immerse myself in my crime book again, and hence into stories of intrigue and murder. As much as it is possible to immerse oneself at all into such banalities, while a child is in danger somewhere out there.

It doesn't work.

I would much have preferred to be running around and looking and asking and snooping. The wait is terrible. But Jonson has strictly forbidden me to go anywhere.

And Alex also! He has really threatened what he would do to me, if I now...

So, I can do nothing but somehow try to take my mind off things. And here, at least, we are staying in Ambergris Cay, close to Ana's bar.

But maybe I can still help. And again, my thoughts turn to Sabine.

"The poor child. Where could she be? I have quite a strong feeling that Sabine is still alive," I mutter to myself.

"What did you say?" Alex shouts, as he always does when he is wearing earphones and thinks others can only hear as little as he can.

"I was saying..." I tilt my head at an angle and listen. "Did you hear that?"

"I didn't hear anything at all, but, you know, with these earphones..."

But now we both hear a clear knocking sound.

Frightened, I jump up. Who can this be? Surely, Jonson or his men would shout or radio us before they come onto the boat?

The criminals? The fear is tying a knot in my throat. I really start feeling nauseous. Have I committed a gigantic error with my premature decision to get back on the boat? We stare at each other, but as usual my reasonable Alex has a logical explanation.

"Why would criminals knock first?"

"Sabine," I whisper.

We storm outside, look over the rail and pull a soaking wet, scared Sabine aboard via the bathing ladder. Quickly, we help the girl into the boat.

"My goodness Sabine, where have you come from?"

What a question! While Alex makes tea and I undress the girl, dry her and wrap her into warm clothes, Sabine, stammering, tells the dreadful story about the awful events this evening in the bar.

"Mum's surely desperate, and Ana, if she's still alive?"

And how she herself, Sabine, now only wanted to go home.

And poor Kati, now she will never come back again.

Sabine cries and speaks and cries and cannot stop any more. Quite firmly, I wrap the shaking girl into my arms.

After we have both tried to comfort Sabine in vain, we let the girl lie down and weep. Carefully, I put a blanket over her and confer quietly with Alex about what we should do next now.

"Anyway, you were right," Alex says and looks at me blankly. "You witch with your hunches."

Then he puts his arm around my shoulder and presses me against him. I am starting to believe this is slowly becoming a habit.

"And now, Mrs. Clairvoyant, what should we do?"

Pondering, I look at Sabine, think about it and say, "We can't go ashore here in any case. Not only Jonson is looking for Sabine, that's for sure...and waiting till tomorrow also seems to me to be too dangerous. Now that it's quite late and very dark, I think we should quietly lift the anchor, without putting any lights on, and then go over there, directly to the beach at the hotel, without the engine and only under sail — do we have enough wind?"

Checking, I look out of a hatch and then look round to Alex. But what do I still need to explain to Alex? He has already gone up and it sounds like he is starting to lift the anchor by hand — as the electric winch would make too much noise.

"So much for good advice from a clairvoyant!" I think angrily.

Sabine wants to come up and help us sail to the resort.

"Stay down, Sabine. Keep calm. We'll do this. Don't be afraid."

The girl looks dreadful. Her long hair is a tangle of strands stuck together, her skin is pale and sallow and her eyes look at me fearfully. Quickly, I take the child into my arms and squeeze her. "It will be all right, my girl. Believe me."

Now, I fill her teacup again and pass it to her. A look into her face shows me that Sabine has calmed down a little bit. She reaches for the tea and drinks with small sips. Then, she nods.

So, I extinguish all the lights and go on deck to help Alex.

It's so darned slow. Link after link runs over the follower and disappears into the anchor locker. Alex works the anchor up with as little noise as possible — and as quickly as this allows him to.

Again and again, I look around anxiously. Would the criminals come follow us? Can somebody hear us?

The anchor is finally up. We secretly sneak along the short distance down to the hotel, only using the headsail. Today, it seems to me that it takes forever. Because the wind has almost died off, it hardly fills the sail. So, we only advance at a snail's pace.

Finally, we reach the beach in front of the hotel facility, where we carefully and quietly let the anchor slide down to the sandy bottom.

Concentrating hard, we listen into the darkness. There is no noise above the water; no sound from the beach. Today, there are no fishermen on the move. All the people at Ambergris Cay seem to have fallen into a deep sleep. And I know that Jonson's people will still be looking for Sabine.

And the gangsters certainly as well!

We confer on how we can best inform Jonson. Via radio is too dangerous; going ashore, too. But we must act fast.

Now that we are so close to completing the rescue, we can hardly hold Sabine back. She simply wants to run off — or more accurately, wants to swim off to her mummy. But Alex explains to the girl how dangerous this could still be, simply to set out into the unknown. Then she grows a little calmer, sits down in the saloon and waits.

Alex goes out with his flashlight and sends the Morse code signal that every yachtsman knows — over to the hotel.

S O S

"What are we going to do if the wrong people see this?" I interject anxiously.

"Can you see, the flashlight is shining its cone directly to the hotel wall where Jonson has his office. And where he is certainly bound to be."

"In the middle of the night?" I ask, worried.

"You think he will really go to bed today?"

He waits for one minute and repeats the procedure.

S O S    S O S    S O S

My goodness, there are so many policemen, why aren't any of them over here looking out the window, I think desperately.

S O S    S O S    S O S

All at once, all the lights begin to come on throughout the whole premises, at the hotel and in the park. Men in uniforms or civilian clothes rush from the house and to the water, and every available rowing boat or pedal boat of the resort is put into the water, so that it soon looks as though a wild flock of ducks has taken flight. Then the police motorboat is also finally under way. From here, with the help of my binoculars of course, I can see Jonson personally steering the sleek boat towards us. He gets ahead of all the other boats and, while still quite far off, he shouts out, "Is she there? Is Sabine with you?"

We laughingly confirm the good news.

I never saw anybody climb onto our sailboat quite so fast. "How wonderful that our hopes have now come true!"

He almost slithers down the companionway into the boat in order to see with his own eyes what he almost does not dare to believe.

But there she is in front of him, pale and exhausted, but very much alive — the girl, Sabine.

# It is not over yet

We accompany Sabine and the whole crowd of policemen to the shore and are received there by Sabine's overjoyed parents, a lot of hotel guests and employees.

On the arm of her mother, Sabine hurries off to look for Ana. We all run along behind. In the restaurant, we find Ana with a huge bandage on her head, but otherwise alive and smiling.

"Hello, Indian, it looks good on you, your turban," says Sabine and embraces Ana warmly.

"Yes, you can laugh, you're not the one who's hurting. And now that everything is over, you can be really silly again, can't you, Baby?"

But Ana is not angry at Sabine. She laughs loudly with her resounding voice and presses Biene to her big bosom. You can tell by looking at her, she is so relieved that her protégée was found healthy and in one piece. "So you fled to the sailboat of these people from Switzerland. And all the time," she laughs in my direction, "she suspected you were with me."

Sabine says to Ana, "And she sung a song for me, so that I knew that the sailboat was nearby — as a rescue point. It was a children's song about a boat lying on the shore. I was locked up in the cupboard and couldn't see anything."

But Ana does not understand about the song, "But the main point is, it was useful. And everything has turned out all right."

Sabine is sitting between her mummy and Ana.

And right next to them, Jonson sits attentively. He wants to grant the girl a few moments of happy greeting. He is in radio contact with his men, who are guarding and monitoring the entrances and the hotel area.

He is vigilant, because the danger is not yet completely over.

Sabine must now report to us about her escape, of course. Her gaze wanders into the distance, it's as though everything is running like in a movie before her eyes.

Her face grows serious and, in her now monotonous voice, I can hear the fear, the desperation.

"We ran for our lives," she starts off. "We just knew that we should never have found these drugs. That the men would have to catch us and silence us. Would have to kill us. We ran, but Kati tripped. I wanted to turn back, to help her …she was already lying on the ground, the men all around her. With sticks they…Kati…had no chance."

Now the girl cries violently. As soon as she has calmed down again somewhat, she continues. "I ran and ran. Then, suddenly, I couldn't go on any more, which was when I crept somewhere underneath the thick bushes. It was getting dark. I was absolutely frozen. The fear…and the torture…my thoughts kept returning to Kati…I already knew then that she was dead. I had no doubt that the men would search for me until they found me. They could not let me get away. And then the same would happen to me as it had to Kati."

She thinks of her friend and the tears start streaming down again.

Ana puts her fat arm around Sabine. Her mother takes her hand.

"I squeezed myself tightly into the bushes. But I knew I wouldn't be able to count on being safe there. I knew the only possible way out for myself would be to be get myself among people, but the way to the hotel, or into the village, was too long and certainly would have long since been blocked by men looking for me.

Through the bushes, I could see lights, the multi-coloured lighting of your bar, Ana. You of all people, Ana, whom we were still mocking the day before. How temptingly near you now were, there with the multi-coloured lights — in the bar."

Sabine smiles broadly at Ana. "Your thousand coloured lamps flashed so promisingly to me. So, I didn't think about it any longer and sprinted across the courtyard, through the door and into the tap room. There, I crept under a table."

Addressing us, she says, "I was terribly afraid. What if she now betrayed me? Was it right for me to come here? But I had no other choice."

Sabine considers this, then nods and says, "Probably this was the only right decision. Ana took me into her arms and started to comfort me, saying that all was now well, that I was safe here and I should tell her what had happened. This funny dialect gave me some trouble, but I understood the sense of what she was saying. And it really comforted me."

Sabine takes a sip, thinks about it and then also remarks, "I thought that when Ana knew it was to do with drugs, she would not want to help me anymore. But she did help me. She comforted me and fed me. And she hid me...she helped me despite putting herself into mortal danger. You know the rest."

We are all sitting round the table and have become very pensive. We still have many questions for Sabine, but now Jonson finally interrupts.

"I don't want to bother you," he says, "but I have a few questions that I must first clear up with Sabine. She must describe the men."

He looks at me, "And then I want to speak with you, too."

However, he first takes Ana with him, so that immediately afterwards, as he says, she could go to bed. In a nice hotel bed, safe and secure.

"You stay here tonight too," he decides about us.

He sends Sabine to her room with her parents.

"You take a nice bath, lie down for a while and…stay in your room until I send for you."

"It would be good if I accompany Sabine and…guard her," I whisper to Alex, and then I leave him behind in the restaurant and hurry after Sabine.

While an exhausted Ana is being questioned in the police office, an equally tired Biene sits in the hot tub, lets her mum soap her back and wash her hair and tells her the whole nasty story. I assist them, and so, hear Sabine's dreadful adventure. Her relief about her own rescue is clouded because she now starts talking about Kati. Quietly, she starts to cry.

"It's terrible and I'm so sorry for her parents," her mum agrees. "They came here with the same hope as us, only to discover that their child had been found dead. They are now back home with poor Kati, but in spite of their grief, they think of calling here and asking about you."

And as though this thought had been carried across the wide seas, the phone in the room starts to ring. It is actually Kati's mum from Stockach. Mrs. Keller tells her the good news about Biene being found, but she obviously finds it difficult to speak of her happiness. Biene and I listen tensely.

"At least Biene can describe the nasty criminals who have done this to Kati."

"Yes, certainly we will stay until all of them have been found…"

"No, Biene has not done that yet. She is here and must first …"

"Yes, totally exhausted…"

"Yes, she will then immediately go back downstairs and give the descriptions to the police chief."

"Yes, we think so too."

"It won't be easy for her because she is still terribly afraid. But she wants Kati's killers to be caught as much as we do."

"I will tell her, yes, goodnight."

Biene puts on fresh clothes, calls out to her mother that she is going to quickly call on Duky and then slips out the door.

I jump up as though I had an electric shock, for I suddenly remember that Duky was also on my list of suspects. Because he has been wheeling and dealing with Mel David, the village policeman. Because he needs money.

On the way to the bar, it occurs to me that I must inform Jonson.

Amazing! I can run *and* think at the same time after all!

I turn back in a hurry and make the detour to Jonson in the hotel office. I whizz past an astonished official, two chambermaids and Hal, the hotel manager, along the long hallway…my goodness, this is taking way too long, down the staircase…and push open the door.

Loudly, I call into the room, "Biene is with Duky!" and already run back again.

Jonson is behind me. And then behind him there are two of his people.

We find Duky and Sabine in a small room behind the bar ,that he uses as a warehouse and office.

The barkeeper is just in the process of passing to Biene a glass filled with a colourful drink and says, "Take this now... and you haven't yet seen Jonson?

Sabine's startled eyes stare at the face of Duky, that has been tensed into a grimace.

It is an everyday scene. A bartender passing his guest a glass. And yet, I am also shocked by this harmless scene, distorted now into an act of horror.

Jonson shoots past me, beats the glass from Duky's hand, twists his arm behind his back and hands him over to his people.

To another official, he gives the order to gather up the remainder of the drink carefully and to have it examined.

Jonson looks at Biene, shakes his head in bewilderment and whispers, "As much luck in the midst of misfortune as you're having, this is almost impossible. Please, don't push your luck too much. At some point, even your lucky stars will not be there anymore, either."

He takes Sabine by the arm and leads her out of the small room.

"I've been stupid," Sabine whispers, "and for so much stupidity one should be punished, I know."

"Hopefully not, at least not as long as I'm responsible for you, please!"

He smiles at her, "Come on now, you lucky child."

Jonson grabs the shaken girl even more firmly by the elbow, and does not let go of her again until we are all sitting safely in his office.

Duky is taken away by two men, and while leaving, I hear him cursing quietly but dreadfully.

Jonson turns to me. "I have also almost been punished for my stupidity; for my stupidity in ridiculing your suspicions. Anyway, I have already followed up on it, and I have also checked into everything. But I did not take it too seriously, the thing with the three names on the list."

After Sabine has recovered from this new and hopefully last fright, she starts to report everything about her bad adventure. She describes the men in the bay, the policemen, reports about Kati's death and her own escape.

She tells about her hiding place with Ana, about the fact that, suddenly, this had also not been safe anymore, because these men came and Biene reported about the children's song. Also, she tells about the renewed escape to the sailboat and, finally, the happy return to the resort.

"And where," asks Jonson, "were you after the escape from the bar. Before you swam out to the sailboat? We turned over every stone, searched everything..."

"I crept into the bushes...wanted only to get away from the house. I...wanted to get to the sailboat. Then came one of the men, he was already very close. I would never have made it across the beach. I...I spotted a hole in the ground. It was a small cave, where the slope behind the house drops down towards the beach..."

"The water outlet!" Jonson exclaims, surprised. "My men had also searched there."

"I...crawled into it completely...placed sand and leaves over me...it stank dreadfully."

We are astonished. In the emergency, she had done the only right thing.

"Then, when all was quiet I got into the water and on... onto your boat." She looks at me. "Then finally all was well — almost."

Again and again, Jonson interrupts her, speaks in a hurry into the phone, or gives short, precise commands to his men who are located in the hallway outside the office. Also, he receives phone calls, causing him to nod either grimly or look satisfied. Biene's report takes more than an hour and Mr. Jonson is finally content.

Once during this, he gets the notice from Belmopan that Duky's drink, which has been flown by helicopter to the police medical institute, apart from all the good ingredients, contained a volume of rat poison sufficient for an entire legion of rats.

Jonson can finally also give us the good news, however, that the entire local police have now been questioned. The fact that some of them, who have been on the side of the drug lord, are now trying to save themselves a few years of prison by revealing the names of other gang members. So, they can now gradually search for and arrest the culprits.

Sabine should simply remain here at the hotel. It will carry on being guarded very well until there is really not the slightest danger for her. And now the hotel is safe. This Duky was the last of the gang still here.

"For you, too, the hotel is safe," he turns to us, "so we have booked you a room here, because you are not allowed to return to your boat yet."

Again we sit in the restaurant together. It is as if everybody wants to feel the nearness of the others and not be alone somewhere in a room. We treat ourselves to a nightcap.

Sabine is hungry again, and Hal himself gets her a nice snack from the kitchen.

"We must do something for Ana," Biene says to her father while chewing. "She ultimately saved my life, risking her own life in the process. She can't possibly stay here, maybe there is an accomplice or collaborator, who wants to take revenge. And I believe, anyway, that she would much rather live with her sister in Belmopan."

"Has she told you about her family?" I ask smiling and think about the small boy, who resembles Ana so much.

"Yes, Ana did. And, certainly, she would also much rather have a small restaurant than this sordid, ramshackle, sombre bar. Of course, she hasn't said this to me, but I know it. And we must absolutely send her a whole box of strawberries from Germany. I have had a bath in her strawberry bubble bath and I had to explain to her that strawberries taste just like that. Well, maybe not quite as sweet as this pink foam, but similar. Imagine, Dad, she has never eaten strawberries!"

Sabine's father thinks this is just fine and stresses that he is happy to repay Ana in any way he can for her tremendous efforts.

"And," Sabine still adds, "while we are at it, Sandra and Alex, they must receive quite a special present from us! And the song, I mean the words you have rhymed, Sandra, can you write them down for me in my travel diary? Unfortunately, I have forgotten them again. In the midst of all the hustle and bustle."

She smiles at me, but carries on chatting.

Now, she tells us about her hiding place in the whisky cupboard at Ana's.

"Whisky cupboard?" comes simultaneously from different mouths.

"That's right," Sabine reports. "Ana hides her alcohol in a cupboard inside the cupboard, meaning she has a removable wall installed in a wardrobe and behind it she has room — precisely — to hide cigarettes and alcohol.

And now she hid me. If somebody came into the bar I had to hide there quickly and pull the wall in front of me. But on the second night, a neighbour came and warned us that some men knew about the cupboard and were immediately coming to us. Imagine our fright. The neighbour hid me in a refuse bin until the men had gone again..."

"You poor child," Biene's mum strokes her hand.

"...and afterwards, Ana took out two boards in the second cupboard once again and I had to creep into the narrow passage and practically squat in the pitched roof. She gave me food and something to drink.

Then she nailed the boards up tight, stacked her treasures in front of it, closed the whisky cupboard and drove to Belmopan to finally deflect suspicion from her house."

Mum pats her hand again and Dad declares "Ana that was really courageous…"

"And very wise…diverting suspicion from the bar like that, after hiding Sabine," I throw in.

"We will help her to open her restaurant."

Now, Jonson joins our group and orders himself some food. "Doesn't matter what, just a bit of meat and vegetables" he says. He discusses a few more unclear points with Sabine, and again, urges her not to go out of the hotel, for though all the gang members were in custody, there were unfortunately still collaborators and accomplices who would maybe try to do something to turn matters around for them.

"The men who broke into Ana's house shortly before our arrival were a neighbour of Ana and his colleague. Neither of them gang members, but they wanted a lot of money. The neighbour, Ron, had tried to beat out of his wife, Janet, what she knows about the matter. Because Janet didn't reveal anything, he half beat her to death. They had to take the injured woman to hospital. Well, she's rid of the man now, for many years, at least."

"And? Did she know something?" Alex asks.

"At first, she certainly did. She also warned Ana and Sabine. But later? Then she herself no longer believed that Sabine was still at Ana's. Oh, I don't know. Maybe there was still such a suspicion with Janet, just as with this lady from Switzerland, as Ana so nicely puts it."

Jonson grins at me. "Yes, you, with your — suspect everything and know nothing."

"And get involved everywhere," Alex grumbles.

Now, Jonson reaches into his briefcase, gets out a strange sketch and lays it between us on the table. We stare at this drawing and I look at Jonson. He eats in peace until his plate is empty and then leans back.

"Is this really — what I think — it is?" I gulp.

Jonson nods, "That's clear, right?"

It resembles a little my sketch that I had drawn of the Yank's boat. But here it is much more detailed, and more informative. There are several things on it that I have no idea what they could be.

"Take a look. Here's a big boat, then the small one, on which the two stick figures are unloading boxes." He moves his skinny black finger over the drawing. "You, Sabine, know about one of the boxes. And you, Sandra, know the boat."

He doesn't expect any answer, either from Sabine or from me.

"And here, the two women or girls, one with flowing hair, as if she was running at racing speed…"

"That's me," Sabine whispers, "and there on the ground …"

"Yes," Jonson says quietly, "Katharina, and next to her an open box full of small bags."

"That was our…misfortune, that we found this box. And Kati…"

Now, Jonson draws a complete circle with his finger over the drawing. "We've now caught all these people. The drug boat was stopped in Mexico."

"Aha …," I say and throw a quick look towards Alex.

Had I properly understood the context of Hansi's story and our observations at Cay Caulker.

"Exactly," Jonson says, "the crew of the motorsailer from Cay Caulker. Your statement and the sketch are sufficiently clear to be considered as evidence against the "Amigo." And by the way, the photos that you took at Cay Caulker, though they are dark and out of focus, are still, however, clear enough as evidence."

"Who were these people on the Amigo?"

"The owner is an American, the dark-haired man Guatemalan and both young people are Germans from Hamburg; siblings. They were probably a little unlucky. They were making a tour of America and, in the first week, they were persuaded by the skipper of the Amigo to go on a sailing trip…"

"Why was that? They seemed totally unsuitable to me."

Jonson laughs. "They were. They were to take over the kitchen on board. But, as I heard myself, any food was sent back overboard through them vomiting. The skipper is a hard-nosed crook and has operated in the drug business for some time. He probably believed that if he had such a harmless crew on board, he would not stand out. Wanted to look like a tourist boat as camouflage."

Jonson looks again at the drawing and continues, "Also, the men in the small boats have been nailed and we also have the scattered assistants — almost everybody. This fine gentleman there with the money bag beside him, who is drawn in up there on the big house, this is the boss of the whole evil operation. Our American colleagues caught him at the airport in Miami."

"He's wearing a funny hat."

Jonson laughs. "I also had to brood at length about this. However, this hat is a helmet like the Spanish conquistadors used to wear. The illustrator has done this wisely. He wanted to inform us that the rich gentleman on the roof is a Spaniard."

"And who, I mean, where does this sketch come from?" I ask, surprised.

Jonson smiles sadly. "The sketch was made by a member of the gang. By Ashton, the fisherman…"

"Ashton, the quiet man from the police office?" I ask in amazement.

How it all so slowly fits together into a perfect picture. Like individual pieces of a jigsaw puzzle, to form a big drug-crime picture.

Three pieces for the Yank's boat: we saw it at Cay Caulker, it was caught at Isla Mujeres and it is drawn on Ashton's sketch.

Three pieces for Ashton: at the police station he told of the lost box, he saw his drowned colleagues at the city dock and now his drawing explains the relationships.

Many pieces about the Chief of Police, Mel Davis: in the small bay he was after the girls, with us on the boat he became angry and threatening, in the village he was with Ashton, and in other respects, he has been involved everywhere as well.

Sabine and Kati: over and over again, there are pieces of the jigsaw puzzle with the two girls, who got involved in an evil story by some sort of fluke and only because of this, got things rolling.

So, Ashton has made this drawing. "But…," I ask thoughtfully, "but why didn't he simply write that such and such had done this and that? Why this sketch?"

"They told me Ashton couldn't read and write." Jonson nods contemplatively.

"Yes, he was a good fisherman who knew this region precisely. He could tell the gang where they should search for the final lost box. And so, without knowing it, he put the girls at risk."

"Who said that?"

"Another man from the gang. He said that after the "Amigo" had let the boxes down into the water and they searched in small boats to get them together again, they were simply no longer able to find one of them. On that day in the office, Ashton was not able to say exactly how the box ended up there at Ambergris Cay with the current and with the high tide."

"But during his statements at the police station, he never looked at the map. Always only into the air or at his hands."

Jonson points to the drawing. "I was told he couldn't read any cards, but he had the sea and the tides in his heart, the tide times and currents in his head. He made the sketch just before he rowed out to sea. Only his rowing boat was found. He was a man with many problems and a bad conscience, and he couldn't read or write."

Jonson points to the bottom of the drawing. "At the bottom there, that is supposed to be him. His wife said it's as clear as a photo."

We bend over the paper. At the lower edge of the sketch, a stick figure can be seen with fuzzy hair and big eyes. Yes, that was what he looked like, the kind Ashton from the police station.

From his boat, an arrow points into nothingness.

Jonson nods. "Actually a nice person, I'm told, but unstable. There was all that money and he could not resist it. Wanted to have something to offer his family. Even though he had lost his only son to drugs."

Jonson, sighing, folds up the drawing and puts it back in his briefcase. "It's usually about the money! The people here have so little."

He adds still more. "Unfortunately, the sketch only arrived here late and by detours; almost too late. The leader of the gang was almost able to escape. A few members have fled to Mexico."

He taps on the briefcase and says to Sabine, "I will let you have a copy if you want."

Sabine's mum wants to protest, but Sabine interjects, "Yes, please, this sketch...with Kati on it...yes, I would like to have it. Thanks."

Sabine spoke very quietly, seriously and sadly.

I think to myself that Sabine has certainly lost some of her carefree and childlike high spirits with this experience. She now seems so serious and mature to me.

"And the police chief of the village, this Mel David," says Jonson with a sombre face, "he was actually the one that you recognised in the uniform, Sabine, and the one that you, Mrs. Sassi, have seen everywhere — he has avoided justice. My men found him at home. He had shot himself with his service pistol."

"In his flat?" I ask.

"In his flat, with the view of the whole village!"

"He was up there at his window?" I start feeling all weird. "So, he had been able to overlook the bar and the street from the upper floor of his apartment! And he was halfway to the hotel."

I'm getting really sick at the thought that Sabine had simply fled from the house and might just as well have run in the direction of the street or the resort. Right in front of Mel David's eyes. And his gun! Almost everything would have been in vain.

# One who meddles

We would rather sleep on our boat and in our own bed. But Jonson has only permitted this after we have accepted a two-person guard, who settle down in the cockpit.

"We don't want to risk anything, revenge or whatever. There may still be people here. Though we have arrested pretty much everybody from San Pedro, some of the accomplices are still missing."

So we go, well-guarded, calmly onto the Seeschwalbe.

In the late morning, Jonson comes out to the Seeschwalbe and hands me a copy of Ashton's sketch.

"As a souvenir," he says, "and in appreciation of the help. You saved Sabine. In fact three times — if I may say so. First, the song, so that Sabine knew where she could escape to, then with the actual rescue when you came here with Sabine – and, of course, you too," he nods over to Alex. "And finally," he hesitates, "finally, once more. When you learned that Sabine wanted to quickly take a drink in the hotel bar and I ran after you. That was a damn close call."

He sighs, then goes on, "Oh! Something I would still like to know. What actually happened, with this guy in the village? The guy who threatened you."

"What guy?" asks Alex nonplussed, between us.

I am a little ashamed, and hesitate to get the words out, "Oh, nothing of importance Alex. But when I ran after Sandy – well — when I was watching Sandy, there came this gigantic guy and...I was really afraid."

"You were pursued — and you've said nothing to me about this!" nags Alex.

"Let this go now, it's not important anymore."

"No longer important! I have to say!"

Ungraciously, I wave it off and turn to Jonson. "Do you know something about this...wicked...?"

"Was this maybe a beefy black guy with a mop of curly hair?"

"Yes,...and lightning tattooed on his chest."

Jonson laughs out loud.

"Lightning, the good Lightning. He is head over heels in love with the lovely Sandy. And defends her up to the last. Therefore, no-one in the village has ever dared to reveal something about her child. The lightning! By the way, this great lightning on his chest is not a tattoo, but is freshly painted on again by the quirky guy every morning with paint. With neon paint! And everybody just calls him "Lightning."

Jonson looks at me surprised, "And he had you in his control?" As if he was afraid he would discover some wounds on me.

Now, even I laugh. "I gave him one in his...hmm, yeah...so that he certainly saw another thousand flashes."

Jonson shakes his head and grins, and then he says goodbye with a warm handshake, warns us again to remain on the boat under the protection of his people. He wants to give us the all-clear himself in this case.

"What does that mean?"

"When everybody is caught — really, all the criminals!"

I now like Jonson a lot again. His dark face is beaming with joy, his black African eyes are shining and his handshake is once more really energetic.

He gives the urgent order to both his watchmen to keep a good lookout, and jets back to the shore again in the police boat.

So, I make a late, but extensive brunch for all four of us and a relieved Alex opens a bottle of good champagne — one for special occasions — for all of us to toast the well-survived adventure.

"Once again, we have been lucky, but as of now, effective immediately, no more spying, ever again. Promise?"

Quietly, I smile to myself. I don't want to promise anything. I will always remain the same. Someone who is interested, who interferes, and if possible — helps.

The two policemen are on duty and are unfortunately not allowed to touch the champagne.

"What does that mean, unfortunately?" grins Alex and pours a generous glass for himself. But the young men help themselves with great pleasure to the bacon and eggs, toast, slices of salmon, avocado cream and fruits. As soon as I then spread out the dessert on the small table, our last stock of chocolate from Switzerland, everything is soon eaten up.

"Cheers, witch!" Alex smiles and his left eyebrow shoots upwards, which makes me laugh.

It surprises me a little, however, that he does not still get angry afterwards because of my spying with Sandy and because I have endangered myself with this gigantic guy Lightning. He just says, "You have obviously hidden that from me very wisely," but it sounds unusually genial.

I'm dead tired.

The night has been much too short. After breakfast, I want to go back to sleep for a while, but Alex wants the most precise explanations from me about everything that I suspected, grasped intuitively, pieced together and hexed.

So, I tell him everything in a few scanty words: My suspicions and the questioning in the village; The wrong tracks, like, for example, with Sandy; The list of my suspects that I gave to Jonson; The observation of the bar with the binoculars in the middle of the night; The investigations in the store; My combination.

And the quite strong supposition or intuition that Sabine is in the bar and in mortal danger.

Thus, the most important and most logical thing followed, my song, the message to Sabine.

"Could you be so sure that it was all so?"

Haltingly, I confess, "I was never certain of course. But after I suspected that she was there, it was suddenly logical. The only house with a cellar and rooms under the roof. Except, of course, the police building and the store, but she was certainly not there. And all the other houses…huts had been quickly searched by the police and also hardly offered any hiding places. This was followed by the unusual behaviour of this Ana and her honest, helpful nature."

I think about it and shrug my shoulders, "And then one thing just followed the other, and I thought that if Sabine was hidden there, she simply would not dare to leave the house. Because the way to the resort was so long and dangerous. And Ana did not know, of course, whether she could trust anyone other than the state police. So, she went to Belmopan to make a phone call, in order to speak directly and only with Jonson. It was not only the people that she mistrusted, even the phones here in the town were not safe to her. Ana also suspected the police chief of the village of supplementing his salary with dishonest dealings, as she informed us during her visit to the boat. Why shouldn't that be the drug trade? And Ana knew that he was living in the area and could observe her very well. Herself, her bar and all the way up to the resort. Yes, that is roughly what I was thinking about."

Then I quietly add, "And, nevertheless, it almost went wrong. The men almost got her, and, also, the police chief almost from his window. But, because of this, I made up the song as the last way out for Sabine, and so, I wanted to remain near the village with the sailboat and return to the boat in the evening. And lo and behold, Sabine appeared."

During my report, Alex initially shakes his head disapprovingly. Then he looks at me searchingly, but at the very end, he asks with amusement about the song.

And I start to sing, "I have a tiny little boat!"